# Of Dungarees, Wellies, & Wedding Dresses

## ALEXA MILNE

# About This Book

My name is Chrissy Wychling. I'm a recently divorced clothes designer and tailor in my mid-thirties. I've recently made a momentous decision and moved from Kent to the Yorkshire Dales to start a new business selling wedding dresses for larger brides. I didn't come to this new place looking for love, or even a relationship, but then I met Beth, and a whole new world of possibilities beckoned.

My name is Beth Nethering. My family has farmed this land for hundreds of years. As a child, I dreamed of getting away, and I did. I went to university, found a great job, got married, and had a child. I had my life mapped out then, ten years ago, everything changed. I made some tough decisions. I moved back to the family farm with my daughter then I set about rescuing the place. Now, we milk sheep not cows, we have glamping pods for tourists, and I've just rented the barn to Chrissy who sells wedding dresses. Me, I'm more used to wearing dungarees and wellies. I'm surprised but strangely flattered when Chrissy flirts with me. It's only a bit of fun, isn't it?

*This story is dedicated to anyone who has taken a risk, or anyone who has taken a leap in the dark, and found love where they least expected it, because you never know just who is going to rock your world.*

# 1. Chrissy

"You're going where?" Rob glared at me from the other side of my bedroom.

"I told you. I'm going to the Yorkshire Dales to view new premises." I carefully folded the rest of my clothes into the suitcase.

"But, but…" my brother spluttered. "But that's hundreds of miles away from here. What do you know about the Dales other than what you've seen on the telly? I mean it's practically Scotland—"

"Except for the whole of Northumbria and County Durham standing in between." Geography had never been Rob's strong point.

"You know what I mean. We're in Kent, the furthest south you can get, where you've lived all your life. Do Mum and Dad know?"

I sat on the bed and stared at him. "I'm thirty-five, Rob. I'm divorced. I have my own business, and I have the proceeds from selling what was my marital home. I don't need to get their approval."

"So, you haven't told them."

"No. Not yet. They'll think I'm having a breakdown after... well, everything. I'll tell them, if this place is right." I closed the case.

"You still haven't explained why there."

I sighed. I had lots of reasons, one of the main ones being it was hundreds of miles away from my cheating ex-wife and shop assistant. "You know since you and Ingrid got married, I've been stocking dresses in larger sizes because there's a market out there?"

Rob nodded. "She'd been so upset going from shop to shop. I will always be grateful to you. The dress was gorgeous, and she shone that day."

"I know. So, I researched online, and I've decided to specialise in wedding dresses for the larger figure, but there's already a stockist around here, and we're near enough to London for people to travel there. But there's nothing in that part of the north, at least not a place which specialises. The premises are near a village called Netherington, which is a fifteen-minute drive from the M1. Women could travel from all parts of Yorkshire and Northumbria, as well as Cumbria, Lancashire, and even Scotland. Think of it, Rob. If I can make this place a destination, I could make so many women happy."

Rob grinned. "And we know how you like to do that."

"Piss off." I gazed at my twin. We'd always been close. "This is an adventure for me. Except for university, I've never lived more than ten minutes from home"—*and you*—" Something which annoyed the hell out of Molly. She said I was a stick-in-the-mud with no ambition tied to my family's apron strings. So, I've decided I need a drastic change of scenery."

"Okay, so what is this place you're visiting like?"

I took out my phone. "Here. I'll show you the details." Rob moved to sit next to me. "It's on a farm."

"Did you say a farm—an actual farm?" Rob stared at me.

"Yes. I did."

"A farm with animals and shit, and you want to sell wedding dresses there."

"Lots of farms diversify now, Rob. You've watched *Countryfile*. This place is a converted barn, and it's perfect. It has its own entrance off the road. The interior is L-shaped and flexible. It's got space for storage, changing rooms, bathroom facilities, and a showroom. All I'll need to do is put in partition walls to create separate areas. There's disabled access as well. Lots of people come to holiday in the area, and the farm has glamping pods on site, and offers a honeymoon getaway. If I can show them I can complement them as a business, it'll help. People will come to me for a dress, and I can show them how beautiful the area could be for a visit. Apparently, the village church is popular for weddings. I've sorted a loan with the bank, and I can advertise for staff locally. I need this to work."

Rob checked out the photographs. "I have to say it looks good. I was expecting something wooden with a thatched roof, not this. It's certainly big enough. The farm's website is good too. It says they rear sheep for milk—that's different. You'll need a website yourself for the new place. I suppose you'll be expecting mate's rates?"

"I'll be expecting I'm-your-twin-sister rates. I'll need to advertise for an assistant too. I have a list of jobs."

"You do know the family will want to visit."

"They can stay on the farm."

"I can't see Mum and Pops going for glamping, no matter

how glamourous it is. Which reminds me. Where will you live? Or haven't you thought of that?"

I elbowed his arm. "I've thought of it, thank you. It's the low season, so I'll probably be able to rent a property until I get something more permanent sorted." I glanced at my watch. "Right, I need to get going. I'm staying at a pub in the village tonight, and it's a long drive. Keep your fingers crossed the motorways are kind."

Rob hugged her. "Ring me. And take care on the road. I know you can drive but it's the idiots I worry about."

"I will. And you know you're always the first to get my call." As twins we'd shared all our decisions and even had our own special language as children. Rob hugged me again. I'd miss him.

"I hope you find what you're seeking, sis."

Later, washed and refreshed after several hours of driving, I sat on a stool at the bar of the inn and glanced around. Despite the time of year, the place was busy. In summer, I guessed the inn would be packed with visitors. Every now and again someone looked my way, probably wondering who the stranger, dressed rather unconventionally, was sitting amongst them. The space had seating of every kind, unmatched chairs, old church pews, even some made out of barrels with cushions on top—it had an old-fashioned charm. The room was long with a welcome roaring fire at each end. The wooden bar gleamed. I ran my hand over the grain, feeling each knot.

"It was allegedly made from one long oak tree over two hundred years ago or came from one of the ships decommissioned after the battle of Trafalgar—take your pick. There are lots of stories about this place. It's been here in one form or another since the early seventeenth century." A bartender appeared in front of me with a welcoming smile.

"It's beautiful," I said.

"Thank you. Now, what can I get you? We have all sorts."

I gazed at the rows of spirits on offer. "Gin and tonic with a slice of lime if you have such a thing."

"We do. And will you be eating with us tonight?"

I'd noticed the more formal restaurant when I'd come down from my beautifully appointed room. "Yes, so if I could have a menu."

The bartender produced one with a flourish. "Everything is available, and there are specials on the board. As much of our produce as possible is sourced from within the Dales."

"That's good to know." I perused the menu, surprised at how hungry I felt. *It must be all this clean country air or the long drive.* Jan, according to his name badge, placed a large drink in front of me complete with the desired slice of lime. He served someone else then returned.

"What can I get you?" Jan brandished a notebook along with a beaming smile. I had no illusions this flirty demeanour was meant just for me, and anyway, I was probably ten years too old for him, and if he was really interested then he was barking up the wrong tree.

"Everything sounds so lovely, but I'll have the shepherd's pie please."

"An excellent choice. And filling if you're not having a starter. The meat comes from a few miles along the road at the Nethering Farm.."

Jan returned and busied himself with the other customers while I sipped my G&T. Nethering Farm was my destination. I caught Jan's eye when he'd finished serving.

"Strangely enough, I'm visiting Nethering Farm tomorrow," I said.

"Oh, you must be the person coming to see the barn. My mum went to school with Beth." He leaned forward. "Everyone knows everything around here. You only have to sneeze and someone in the village asks if you've got a cold when you pop out to the local shop."

"The village is Netherington?" I asked. "Not Nethering."

"Yes. The Nethering family have been farming in this area for centuries."

I decided to do a little digging. "And Beth runs the place? Isn't it unusual for a woman to be in charge?"

Jan glanced from side to side. "There's a reason—big tragedy."

An older woman appeared behind him. "Thanks, Jan. Other people need serving. And your food is ready, Ms Wychling. You're on table two in the restaurant near the window if you go through the door to the left."

As I strolled out of the bar, I couldn't help hearing the woman admonishing the bartender in no uncertain terms. "We don't gossip to strangers, Jan. Beth's business is her own to share, not ours."

I took my seat in the dining room. *So, there's a mystery and a tragedy.* A girl brought my food, which gave off a heady aroma, making my mouth water. Thoughts about my prospective landlady could wait for now.

Early the next morning, I entered the dining room again for breakfast. I checked the comprehensive menu and decided a full English would set me up for the day—and a pot of breakfast tea. I didn't function in the morning without at least two mugs of builder's brew.

The older woman from last night appeared to take my order. "What can I do you for this morning?"

"I thought I'd treat myself to the full breakfast, but no tomato."

"Black pudding?"

I thought for a moment. "Yes, why not. I'm not sure when I'll get to eat again today."

"I believe you're interested in the barn at Nethering Farm."

"I am," I said. "I sell wedding dresses for larger women because they deserve to feel as special as any other bride on their big day.

"There are already a few wedding shops in the area, especially in York."

"Yes, but mine will start at a size where most shops finish. No one in my shop will ever stare at a person with an expression which says we have nothing for you. I will always have something, and I can customise any dress."

The woman looked me up and down. I suppose I did appear different from the norm, dressed as I was in a three-piece charcoal grey trouser suit.

"I'm Karen, by the way. Beth and I have known each other practically since birth. I run this place with my husband."

I held out my hand. "It's good to meet you. You've a lovely place here. Jan told me last night it has quite the history."

Karen's expression softened a little. "Thank you. It's taken a lot of work, but George and I are pleased, and customers seem to like it. Can I just say your suit is stunning. Not everyone could carry off such an outfit."

"I studied tailoring at university and make my own. Don't worry though. I've packed my wellies for today. I know what farms can be like."

Karen nodded. "I'll get your breakfast sorted for you."

An hour later, I was on the road again. Karen had given me clear directions because satnavs sometimes took people up the wrong side road. I spotted the farm sign easily then took the first turn on the left. My business sign would need to go there. A few metres later, I pulled up in front of a large stone-built building with a slate-tiled roof and three large windows on the longer side. A woman stepped out of the door. My stomach flipped. My trained eye could imagine her curves, even under her denim dungarees worn over a loose white hoodie. If I had a type, Beth Nethering was that type. And to top off the body, she had thick dark brown hair tied back into a ponytail. She shouted sensible and practical.

*Pull yourself together. You're supposed to act professional not ogle someone who could become your landlady.* I admonished myself then checked my face in the rear-view mirror. I wasn't a great one for make-up and I'd just scraped my hair back into a messy bun, figuring visiting a farm was not the occasion to dress up. After pushing open the car door, I slipped off my driving shoes, grabbed my polka-dot wellies, turned, then pushed my feet and trousers into the protective footwear, even though I had to say there wasn't a hint of anything unfortunate to step into in the gravel-covered parking space.

Beth Nethering met me at the car. I stood and held out my hand. "You must be Beth. I'm Chrissy, Chrissy Wychling. It's good to meet you. I wasn't sure of the terrain, hence the boots. I hope I didn't keep you waiting."

"Karen called me to let me know you were on your way. Nothing much happens around here without someone noticing." We chatted about the journey and the hotel. I was careful to praise the place.

"So," Beth began. "As you can see the barn is substantial, and there's plenty of room for parking. You'll have your own separate entrance, so your customers won't have to come onto the farm. We didn't want to turn it into another house so close to ours, so this seemed the perfect use. The place has undergone significant changes in the last ten years."

"I suppose farmers have to diversify to make ends meet these days."

"We do. If we depended on farming, we wouldn't manage. It's as simple as that." I noted Beth didn't explain further. *Well, she doesn't know me from Adam yet, so fair enough.* "Right. Shall we go in?"

I followed Beth up the ramped entrance, noting the low threshold doors that opened wide enough to let more than one person enter. The space we stepped into was huge.

"As you can see we've left the insides for you to configure, though there is a small kitchen and toilet facilities at the other end. We've made it so people can plan for themselves. I'm not sure what you'll need, but Stan, our builder will sort everything for you. We've added a good security system too, which I'll explain later."

I stepped to the middle of the space and turned slowly, imagining where everything I needed could go.

"What do you think?" Beth's question interrupted my thoughts.

"I need a space for changing rooms, storage of the dresses, and a space for the customers to show off to their friends and family. Prospective brides hardly ever shop alone, and some bring a large entourage. I want this place to be a destination for women in the north. Each visit will be especially for them. Each person will have an appointment though I won't stop people just dropping in. Each will get fitted by me. Each will get advice. Each will be able to feel confident they will get the dress which makes them look as incredible as they all deserve." I stopped.

Beth stared at me, eyes wide, with a blush on her cheeks.

"Sorry. I can go on. My sister-in-law had a terrible experience from haughty women staring down their noses at her until I found a designer who catered for someone her size. I saw the joy on her face the day she first put on the dress, and the same joy the day she wore it to marry my brother." I didn't explain how my ex-wife thought specialising in large sizes was financial suicide.

"I understand," Beth said. "And I think it's a lovely idea. I lost weight to fit into my dress."

"I didn't realise you were married," I blurted out before my brain kicked into gear.

"I'm not. Not anymore. Divorced ten years ago. We still keep in touch, and he does all the farm accounts, but he lives in London with his second wife. Our daughter spends time with him during the holidays."

"How old is she—your daughter?"

"Amy is seventeen going on thirty-five like most teenage girls. Unlike a lot though, she has a sensible head on her shoulders." Beth glanced out of a window. "And she loves this place."

"Just like you do?"

Beth sighed. I have no doubt there was a whole history in that sigh. "Me?" She shrugged. "I grew up hating it. Couldn't wait to get away. But you don't always get what you want from life, do you?

# 2. Beth

I knew Karen would be on the phone the moment Chrissy got back to the inn.

"So, what d'you think? Is she going to take it? I haven't had chance to speak to her since she returned. D'you want me to ask?"

"No, there's no need."

"I can do subtle if that's what you're worrying about." I could hear the huffing in her tone.

"She's already said she wants it. All we need to do is sort out the details."

"That's brilliant. Though I'm not sure about the wedding dress idea. Still, I suppose she knows her market."

The back door slammed, caught by the wind. Autumn was setting in. "Amy's home from school. Why don't you come round tonight if you can be spared?" It had been a while since we'd managed a good gossip.

"I'll make sure I can be spared." I smiled to myself, knowing Karen could never resist, but she'd been a good friend after all that had happened, when not everyone had been so supportive.

"Then, I'll see you later. And I'll bring food."

My daughter entered the kitchen like a hurricane as always, followed by Ralph, her border collie, who'd spent the last thirty minutes next to the front door waiting for her. She slung her coat on the back of the chair, threw her bag on the table, then disappeared into the fridge before emerging with a bottle of water, and drinking at least half.

"Hello," I said after a couple of minutes. "How was school?" We had this conversation every weekday. It could last five seconds or thirty minutes. "Would you like a hot drink?"

She plonked herself on a chair and fussed Ralph. "There's my good boy. Have you been our helping Ned today? Have you been a good boy?" The dog's tail wagged hard against the leg of the table. Now his person was safely home, he could settle into his dog bed until she moved again.

"Can I have one of those frothy coffee things. Mum? The bloody heating was broken on the bus again. I swear that vehicle is older than God. They may as well get a couple of oxen and attach it. We'd be here quicker. And it was the mean driver again. You know, the one who wants us to prove we're still in full-time education, even though we're all wearing uniforms and he's picked us up outside the bloody school."

*Ah. It's going to be one of those days.* I'd need another drink too. The rant continued. I knew my job was to listen, nod, and make the occasional noise in agreement.

"Then we had this supply teacher for maths. I swear I don't know where they find them. We were supposed to be doing calculus, but we knew more than he did. I hope Ms Black is back tomorrow. She may be a tyrant capable of ruling North Korea, but at least she knows what she's talking about. I've a load of biology homework to get done tonight as well, so I'll be out of your hair. Me and Cathy are going to work together online, so the bloody broadband better not be on the glitch."

"It's working fine since the update." I put the mugs down and joined her at the table. "Will you make sure Geoffrey is fed and watered."

She grinned at me. It was the sort of yes-of-course-I-will facial expression any parent would recognise.

"The work experience girl took him out this morning for you," I continued. "She gave him a good gallop."

"Great. I'll remember to thank her, though she usually thanks me for letting her. She's a natural with horses. I'll give him a good ride on Saturday. These bloody darker nights are a nuisance."

"You said you'd take care of him." I stared at my coffee when I spoke, not daring to meet her gaze. She had a lot of her grandmother in her and took no prisoners.

"I know, and I do, but you know what my days are like with sixth form. I get up at the crack of dawn to clear out his stable and make sure I get to school on time. It's not like I don't help around here when I can."

"I know you do, love. And I appreciate it. Farm life isn't easy, and I made the decision to bring you back here." I blew on my coffee and sipped it. "Anything else to report?" I asked.

"Nothing much. Sally and Sam have split up again. It's all drama with those two. Oh, and Dad rang. He wants me to visit at half-term. Is that all right?"

"Of course. You know it's fine. I need to talk to him about the accounts anyway."

"Oh, I nearly forgot. Did the woman come to view the barn?"

"She did. And she's taking it to set up a business selling

wedding dresses. She seems nice." She'd certainly been striking. Not everyone could pull off a three-piece suit, an unfussy bun, and polka dot wellies. "Her name's Chrissy Wychling."

"Interesting surname. I wonder where it's from."

I glanced at the contract Chrissy had already signed. "Her address is in Kent, so she's coming a long way."

"I wonder what or who she's getting away from?" There was my astute daughter again. The thought had crossed my mind.

"Anyway, Mum, I'll take this coffee upstairs. Call me when dinner's ready, will you? And yes, I'll hang my coat up in the proper place and take my shoes off before I go upstairs. Come on, Ralph." The dog jumped up, ready to follow.

"Karen's coming over later. She's bringing food."

Amy chuckled. "Oh good. Something decent for a change."

I threw a tea towel at her. "Ungrateful brat. You could always learn to cook if you're bothered. I did make a fresh loaf this morning, and there's always ready meals from the farm shop."

She disappeared slamming the door behind her before I could remind her not to.

Karen arrived at seven-thirty on the dot. By then Amy had been out and checked on Geoffrey and I'd banked up the range, checked on the chickens and ducks, and our small herd of cattle, and spoken to Ned about the sheep. Sheep were our main income source A few of us local farmers had joined together to form a local company and now we produced butter, cheese and yoghurt. Selling to a posh supermarket provided a steady income, and along with the insurance gave the farm a level of financial security.

As usual, Karen came in without bothering to knock. We'd

known each other since birth. She'd grown up in the village where her parents ran the local store. They'd retired, but the store continued, run by a couple who'd moved from Birmingham. The village of Netherington had managed to retain its charm. People came to see the castle ruins, and the visit the niche shops. We had a narrow-gauge railway line which attracted people, as well as the gorgeous scenery. Tourists flocked to the place in the summer, and Karen's pub—the White Hart—did a roaring trade, unlike many.

"I bring food," she said, placing a bag on the table. "Stick it in the oven to warm it through. George has made this amazing beef stew with dumplings, and I made one of my sticky toffee puddings." She took everything out of the bag.

I texted Amy to get down for half an hour. "It's easier than yelling up the stairs," I explained.

"You don't have to tell me. I have two children, remember. Jan can't wait to get back to university because we work him too hard, and Claire's had another run-in with her boss today. The woman thinks she's God by the sound of it, and she's always making comments about Claire's appearance. I've told her to take no notice, but she's desperate to find another job in retail."

I put the stew into the oven to warm, then poured a glass of wine for both of us. "I may have the solution to Claire's problems."

"Oh, yes. There's no way Claire would work on the farm."

"I don't mean the farm...well, I sort of do. Anyway, Chrissy, who came to see the barn said she'll need an assistant in the shop, and let's face it, Claire would be perfect. She's got experience in retail and as Chrissy intends to market her dresses at a particular group, she's..." I hesitated.

"What you mean to say is she's more than a size twenty."

"So am I," I said. "I can't remember my exact measurements. It's been years since I worried. I once had someone tell me at university I wouldn't make a good barrister because I didn't have a lean and hungry look about me. I enjoyed beating her later on when my client took hers to the cleaners. Us larger ladies need to stick together. We can't all have the perfect husband who cooks balanced, nutritious meals."

"I know how fortunate I am, though sometimes I long for a crisp butty."

"And he worships the ground you walk on. It was a lucky day when he walked into your store asking for directions."

"It was. I won't deny it. Twenty years on and I have two great kids and we run the best inn around for miles. I'm happy. He's great in the kitchen and incredible in the bedroom. So, what did you think to this Chrissy Wychling, then? I will say she had an interesting dress style. Not every woman can rock a three-piece suit. D'you think she might be gay?"

I snorted. Typical Karen. "Just because she was wearing a trouser suit, doesn't make her gay."

"No. I suppose not. Her hair wasn't short either and she's blonde."

"Really?" I tutted. "For goodness' sake. Not everyone is a cliché. Anyway, I don't care what she is. She's signed the lease and says she wants to move in within the month. She also needs an assistant, which brings me back to Claire. She's selling wedding dresses."

"I know. She told me. Wedding dresses for the larger lady. I think she may be on to something. I've seen these TV shows, and it must be awful if you're big and you want a great dress. I mean larger ladies get married, and people are bigger now. Why shouldn't they have a great experience and more choice?"

"Exactly." Sometimes Karen could live up to the reputation of her name, but she could also be generous, and I knew she'd defended me more than once. Alexa reminded me about the stew. I smiled, waiting for Karen's usual comment.

"Still got the male voice speaking then," she said, smiling.

"Yep. There's nothing wrong with getting to tell a man what to do."

# 2. Chrissy

*A month later*

I sat on the black padded sofa I'd brought from my shop and stared at the chaos around me. Tall cardboard boxes filled so much of the main space, with pieces of furniture scattered throughout. The removals firm had emptied their van and departed, leaving me to deal with everything else. I wanted to run away. No, what I really wanted was someone to wave their magic wand and for everything to be in place before more dresses arrived.

I'd arrived the day before. To my utter amazement, everything I'd planned for the space had been achieved to the letter in four weeks. Clearly, Beth had contacts. Now, my new premises had a changing area, a small kitchen and toilet area, though I'd insisted the toilet was big enough to be used by someone in a wheelchair. There were also well-placed handrails and an alarm and a pull-down baby changing table. They'd moved the wall to make this possible. A compact office had been the compromise. The internet connection was surprisingly good. The other two spaces were for storing the dresses I'd keep on site and the most important space of all—where the bride would show off their dress to anyone here with them, or to themselves. A large circular podium ready for standing on lay against the wall, and somewhere, wrapped in cardboard was a triptych of mirrors I'd ordered.

The main door opened.

"Everything came, then. Wow. This will take a while to sort. I brought coffee and bacon butties. Oh fuck, you're not a vegetarian, are you? No, of course you're not. Mum would have said. Anyway, here you are. We can have these, then get started."

I smiled. "Good morning, Claire." I took the coffee and sipped carefully. It was better than any you'd get from a chain. We'd need a drinks maker here. I made a mental note to ask what machine Karen used at the pub. "This coffee is great, though for future reference, I'm more of a tea drinker in the morning."

Claire took out a small notebook from her pocket. "Duly noted. Now, where should we start. I checked all the rooms yesterday. The builder's done a good job. Mind you. They'd be too scared not to. Mum would have killed him, and Aunty Beth may be on the short side, but she takes no prisoners either."

I'd interviewed Claire online. She had a bubbly, infectious personality some might have found irritating, but her enthusiasm was undeniable. In three weeks, she'd done her research and had listed every wedding fayre within the next six months and within fifty miles—a lot of wedding shops also took their wares out on the road. I'd need to get this new venture noticed. The website was built and ready, and the soft launch was set for Saturday. We had five days to get this place ready for customers.

"Okay," I said, after finishing the bacon butty. "We'd better start with putting the rails up in the storage area, then we can hang up the dresses and steam press them. The drawers are on wheels. In those we keep the extras like lace sleeves and bodices, shoulder netting, all those little additions we can add to a dress to customise it. The shelves are for the shoes and other accessories. We'll need to get more stock in."

"I've been watching shows online," Claire said. "There are so many amazing dresses out there. I think I've learned the names of all the features. I kept thinking what would suit me. I mean I'm taller some at five-foot-nine, but I'm also a size twenty-four."

I cast a trained eye over her. Claire had a pear-shaped figure with most of her weight in the middle around her tummy and hips. She would suit something strapless but with a wide skirt, depending on how bold she wanted to be. I stood ready to get going. "I pride myself I can find a dress for anyone Claire, and if not, then I've been known to get out my machine and make one."

"I never learned to sew at school," Claire said. "And Mum doesn't sew."

"Then I'll teach you."

"I feel like I've such a lot to learn."

"You have. I did a degree in textiles, but it didn't help me to begin with. The biggest skill in this job is matching the dress to the person. Many brides, or more especially their mothers, come in with fixed ideas. Larger brides can lack confidence about their bodies and what they can wear. They may secretly want to try things but be too afraid. We have to discover those hidden desires and help them achieve them or point them in the right direction. I've had brides come in wanting red dresses who've left with something completely different, as well as those who have done the opposite. I make a promise on the website, that whatever the size, I will produce a dress they can wear on their big day that will allow them to be beautiful. We will start at the sizes other shops finish, and the This is Me Bridal Barn will be a destination for brides all over the north and further afield. You and me, Claire will achieve this, and today is when we start."

"I feel like I'm about to go ten rounds in a ring or do one of those tasks on celebrity shows. I don't know whether to be excited or terrified."

We emptied box after box, taking only a brief amount of time for a drink and sandwich. Claire worked her socks off and never complained. By six in the evening, my feet ached, my knees ached, in fact everything ached. I planned on using the hot tub at the glamping pod for the first time, despite the cool weather. Claire sat beside me on the leather bench.

"You have been amazing," I said. "I can't believe we got all those dresses on rails. Tomorrow, we need to sort and steam press, then we need to check out sellers and begin to fill in gaps in our stock at the higher end of the sizes." I checked my phone. "We have a message," I said. "Wow, someone wants to come Saturday morning. Apparently, their wedding is a month away."

"Shit. That's cutting it fine. Can we do it?"

"We'll give it a bloody good try. Tomorrow, the decorator will be here to paint the walls, and I've more seating being delivered along with material to drape. What I need is photographs. The mannequins help, but people like to see real people wearing real dresses to give them ideas. I've a few from my old shop which brides kindly gave me permission to display. We'll get more as we go along. I've ordered banners for wedding fayres, which—fingers crossed—should be here this week too."

"It's all so exciting," Claire said. "I feel like we should smash a bottle of champagne against the walls at the opening."

"Not on my watch. Champagne is for drinking."

"Hello. Anyone in?" I recognised Beth's voice. "We thought we'd come to check things were all right."

The inner door opened, and Beth stepped through wearing her usual dungarees, this time accompanied by a red and white-striped top, followed by a teenage girl who must be her daughter Amy. I had to admit, she didn't look old enough to have a daughter of that age. Beth glanced around. Flattened cardboard lay everywhere in piles.

"You two have been busy. I saw the van unloading the boxes when I was out with the sheep this morning."

"We've hung up all the dresses, Aunty Beth. Some are so beautiful with lace and even feathers. Chrissy is going to teach me how to string a corset tomorrow. You could volunteer to model for me if you want. It would help."

I glanced up at Beth in an attempt to read her reaction. She had the sort of hourglass figure that would suit a corseted dress or just a corset, and maybe stockings and heels, if she ever got out of her wellies. Her expression, however, was inscrutable.

"Your Aunty Beth will be busy. You can practice on the mannequin first, Claire. And it's time you went home."

"Can I show Amy the dresses first?" Of course, they'd known each other for a long time and probably went to school together. They were only separated by four years though, with Amy still in school, and Claire working, the age gap seemed bigger.

"Okay. But remember no touching without the gloves on." They disappeared through the back, leaving Beth and I alone. "Busy day?" I asked.

"Always busy with milking and the lambs to care for. Ours are older and away from their mothers now. Our collective doesn't lamb at the same time of year, which gives us milk at all times, though we keep them longer with the mothers than farms. Luckily, sheep' milk freezes well. Jed does most of the work with his father, Ned."

"Ned and Jed? Really?" I couldn't help laughing. "Do they have shawls and crooks and walk around chewing the ends of wheat stalks?"

Beth smiled. I liked it when she did. She appeared tired, but I guess farming was a tough life.

"Ned's the old-fashioned sort. He and his wife live in a cottage at the edge of our land. How they fitted four children in there, I'll never know. Their youngest, Joe is in Australia working on a sheep farm. Mary works in Brussels advising on agriculture. Alice lives nearby. She married a farmer. Jed lives with his husband in the village. He has a degree in agricultural management, specialising in sheep. He knows everything there is to know about getting the best from them, but he does lots of other jobs around the farm. I'm fortunate to have them both here. When I went into this venture, I knew nothing except we had to change if the farm was to keep going. We didn't make enough from selling the lambs every year and fleeces make nothing. We may be in a niche market, but it's growing."

"I suspect people would see this shop in the same way. My brother thinks I should have all sizes, but I'm determined to start at size eighteen and go upwards. Last year, I had a woman in her sixties come into my shop for a dress. She was renewing her vows. She said when she was young, and a size eighteen, her mother had made her dress because there was so little choice. Now, size eighteen is nothing. You can get it in lots of shops, but size thirty or higher, not so much. I went to the ceremony. She and her husband were an amazing couple—everyone cried. She finally had the dress she'd dreamed of all her life. She's one of the reasons I made this decision."

The inner door to the changing area burst open. I made a mental note to put a rubber stopper on the other side on the wall.

"The dresses are amazing, Mum. They've even some in black. Can you imagine getting married in black with Doc Marten boots? I could ride in on Geoffrey with him being black too. That would be a sight."

"Let's get university over with first, please." Beth glanced at me. Was she hoping for my support?

"I think your mother's right."

Amy gave one of those mischievous grins I guessed her mother often saw. "It's okay, Mum. Don't panic. I don't intend to get married until I'm at least thirty, if then. Still, I would look great in black."

Later, after everyone had gone, I locked up and switched on the security system. As well as an alarm, I had cameras connected to an app on my phone. I needed this business to work with the investment I'd made into it—well, myself and the bank. Molly and I had made a profit selling our house, which helped give me some savings.

It was pitch-black outside, so I was glad of the security lights lining the path to the glamping pods. I found the key and opened the door to the first one. Inside had everything I needed for now. My household goods were still in storage along with a lot of my clothes. Cooking facilities were limited to a couple of rings and a combi-oven and microwave. I opened the small fridge and took out a bottle of water.

*Hot tub or food?* They said you shouldn't swim on a full stomach, so I switched on the water heater, opened the back door, pulled off the covers and hit the switch to make the water bubble. Fifteen minutes later, I lay naked in the warmth, letting the swirl of the water take away the tensions of the day. I made a mental list of tomorrow's tasks, glad I'd given Claire the assistant's job. I had the feeling she would prove to be an asset. My thoughts drifted to my new landlady. Could we be friends? I hoped so. I was a long way from home and all I'd ever known. As usual when I met someone new I wondered about her clothes and if she ever wore anything else than dungarees. As a child, I'd made paper dolls and then designed whole wardrobes suitable for any occasion, now I did the same, ending the collection imagining Beth swathed in a shoulderless midnight-blue velvet dress that accentuated every curve.. I shivered even though the water was still hot then yawned. I needed food then sleep to be ready for tomorrow.

# 4. Beth

After monitoring the sheep in the milking parlour, I decided to take advantage of the dry weather and check the state of the walls after winter. This year the weather had been kinder. The snow showers had come and gone but not settled in any great quantity, which made life easier. We'd kept the sheep in the intake fields or inside the large barn for lambing. Thankfully, the long nights with little sleep were over. This year we hadn't lost any ewes in birth, and the lambs had adapted to being apart from their mothers after sixty days. Only the lambs born to the small groups of endangered breeds stayed outdoors with their mothers. Some days, I'd spend time in the huge barn with the smaller lambs who needed to be fed by hand. Seeing those wiggly lambs' tails would always bring a smile to my face.

After putting fuel in the quad bike, I let Geoffrey into the paddock, collected the eggs, and decided to bring Ralph along for the ride, knowing Jed was too busy to give him a run out with his dogs today. The quick early morning walk he got with Amy was never enough for such an active breed.

"Come on, Ralph."

The border collie rushed out of the house and sat on the back of the quad bike with his tongue lolling out. I didn't drive fast as any bump might send a person and bike rolling over, and I always wore a hard hat. Along the way, I made a note of any gaps in walls and fences before the sheep were let out into fields further from the milking parlour. Grazing sheep needed a large area.

Driving through the yard, I spotted Jed and stopped.

"I'm off to check what repairs we need, and I need air." I'd spent far too much time stuck indoors doing paperwork recently. "There's no point in wasting those dry-stone walling skills your dad taught you. As soon as I've checked, I'll let you know."

"Thanks, Beth. I was about to ask Joe to do the survey." Jed and I were around the same age and had been to school together in the same class at primary level. I was the first person he'd told he was gay.

"Good yield today," he said. "And I've got the details for the course on ice cream-making. All of the farm managers are going. Lars said I've got to bring home samples." Jed had married George Petterson's younger brother ten years ago. By coincidence they'd met at university in York. Lars worked at the Jorvik Exhibition often dressing up as a Viking to take parties around the displays.

"How's our new business owner settling in?" he asked.

"Chrissy? She's hoping to be ready for a soft opening on Saturday. Claire is loving it—says Chrissy is a great boss. My biggest concern is whether she's done her homework setting up here. I suspect she's ploughed a lot of money into starting things for herself."

"Well, you did it. This place would have gone to the wall

and been sold off like so many others if you hadn't made such hard choices. Few people would give up all you did—a six-figure salary *and* a marriage for a farm in the Dales."

It had been a huge decision, but I'd never regretted it except on a few dark nights all by myself when the enormity of what I's done threatened to overwhelm me.

"It'll be good for you having another person around here until she finds a place. You don't get out enough, and just going to the White Hart Inn doesn't count. When was the last time you went to the pictures or even out to dinner? I bet she'll be lonely so far away from home. A girls' night out could be what you need."

I guessed he'd been talking about me with Karen.

"Maybe I could ask her, and you and Lars could join us." He grinned at me then strolled off chuckling to himself. "Right," I shouted after him. "Enough gabbing with you. I'll be off to have a look around."

He waved without turning. Ralph barked at me.

"Okay, boy. I know you want to be out there too."

The day was one of those cool, crisp, bright ones perfect for tramping the footpaths of the National Park. In this sort of landscape, the sheep were often contained in smaller fields enclosed by walls that had existed for centuries, much like my family. Every time I stopped to inspect a section, Ralph jumped from the bike and ran around. With me, he had more freedom. With Amy, it was all about the work. They were a good team and had won a few junior dog trials.

As we opened and closed the gates, I checked on them as well, noting a couple needing repairs because the wood had rotted. Repairs on a farm were constant. On the higher sections, I got off the bike and walked. At the top of the hill, I took the flask of coffee from my backpack and sat staring at the expanse of the dales. It was beautiful. The grass was beginning to grow again—the sun would help. The trees also had started to sprout leaves. A couple of rabbits chased each other in the next field, luckily unseen by Ralph, who was sniffing a tree. The only buildings visible were small stone bothies, shelters used by shepherds in years gone by, dotted the landscape, built next to the dry-stone wall. I sipped my coffee.

As a small child, I'd loved the place, being able to roam around in all this space, but as a teenager I'd resented living on the farm. While those in the towns had the beginnings of social media, we had nothing. I'd planned my escape and achieved it. London had seemed like a different world—so many people and so many buildings—cinemas, theatres, museums, and night clubs. Even getting pregnant and married so soon after graduation, I'd managed or rather we'd managed, and our careers had gone from strength to strength. Graham had been a good dad, and still was a good dad. I'd had my whole life planned out, and then everything had gone to hell in a handcart as Ned would say.

I packed the flask away and headed back down the hill with Ralph at my heels. Ten years ago, I'd made my choice. Did I regret it? Sometimes. But not today. Today, breathing in the crisp, cool air, I couldn't imagine being anywhere else.

"Come on, Ralph." I resisted the temptation to call him Ralphie. Amy said it confused a dog when you used the wrong name. "Do you think I should ask Chrissy if she fancies going to the pictures? I've no idea what's on." I couldn't remember the last time I'd been. "I mean, I don't want her to get the wrong impression."

Ralph barked. I got the feeling I'd been admonished. "Yes, you are right. I shouldn't make assumptions.

Three hours later, I was back at the farm ready for something to eat. Ralph took all of five minutes to eat his bowl of dog food. I half expected to see him chuck it all up again. I ate my soup and homemade roll, left Ralph snoring in this basket, then strolled over to the bridal barn to find Ned loading a large sign onto his wagon.

"I hope you don't mind," Chrissy said. She was dressed in jeans and an Aran jumper with her wellies, and still managed to appear stylish. "I couldn't find you to ask, and I got no answer on your phone. Ned said he'd put the sign up along the road while we wait for the paint to dry in the main room. I wasn't sure if I needed permission from anyone."

"As long as you put it at the corner you'll be fine as that's my land." Sometimes, the park authorities could be difficult, but we could wait and see.

"Thanks, Ned. Will you need a hand? Jed's up sorting out the milk. The tanker's due today."

"No. I'm perfectly capable of managing, thank you. I've got all I need for now. I've me mallet and I can stand in the wagon to hammer it in while the ground is soft from the rain. We'll cement it in when it's drier."

Usually, Ned was a man of few words. His wife, Daisy did all the talking for him as well as making the best cakes I'd ever tasted. What she could do with eggs, flour, and butter. Every year she won prizes at the Netherington village show.

"I'll be off then, Ms Wychling. Please let me know if there's anything else you need doing around the place. And I'll go check on the cattle, Beth. I reckon the cows aren't far off birthing now. You'll have calves for the tourists to gawp at."

Chrissy and I watched the wagon head off through the gate. "Everything all right?" I asked.

"Yes. Ned's been a great help, lifting and carrying, though he doesn't say much. He did bring the most amazing scones and jam—all homemade."

"His wife is a baking goddess."

"Why don't you come in. I could do with a drink. D'you fancy a mug of good Yorkshire tea?"

I rarely turned down tea even though I'd not long had my lunch. Inside, the place appeared much more together. All the boxes had been emptied and more places to sit had been set up. I followed Chrissy into the small kitchen area.

"Watch the walls," Chrissy said. "White is such a dull colour, but it's what is expected."

"Says the woman who sells wedding dresses." Chrissy laughed. She had a nice laugh—the sort that could be infectious.

"I know, but there are other shades available, from black and red to ivory and blush pink. I've a delivery tomorrow, which reminds me, I might need a good dry-cleaning service, one which collects if possible. Do you know of anything?"

"I'll ask Karen at the White Hart. She always knows someone who knows someone."

"We occasionally rent out gowns, so I need to have them professionally cleaned. Not everyone can afford a dress, though I try to keep stock with reasonable prices."

I sat next to the desk. "Getting married is an expensive business. I remember my wedding. My father insisted on paying for everything—said it was a father's responsibility." I'd adored my father and missed his wise advice. No one had been more surprised than me when he and my mum had bought a house in

31

France to retire to, leaving the farm to my brother. We only found out later he'd been advised to slow down for health reasons—and his dicky ticker had taken him from us despite the move.

"What about you? How was your wedding?" I asked when Chrissy handed me a mug.

She looked wistful for a moment. "It was lovely. We got married at a hotel near the beach and had a barbecue afterwards. I wore a teal three-piece suit I made myself—I did tailoring as part of my degree. My partner, Molly wore the dress. It was a perfect day. But not everything perfect lasts."

*So she is gay.* "No, sadly it doesn't." I wanted to ask what had happened but now wasn't the time. "My husband and I were already drifting apart before I decided to return home. We both worked too hard. I had a nanny to take care of Amy, which I hated. We hardly saw each other, let alone had time for our daughter. Now she spends more time with both of us. Graham's remarried and his new wife is expecting."

"And you've never thought about getting married again. Jed seems like a nice bloke." She grinned at me.

"I'll have you know Jed is happily married to a Viking called Lars Petterson."

"Aren't they the people at the White Hart?"

"Lars is George's younger brother. It's a bloody small world around here."

"Oh well. He is handsome though."

*So maybe not completely gay.*

"Have you had any more interest?" I asked changing the subject.

Her face lit up. She had blue-grey eyes like the sea on a cloudy day, whereas mine were boring old brown.

"Yes, we've three booked in for Saturday. We'll stick to bookings when we get established, but for now we need to be ready for walk-ins too. We're coming up to wedding season, so hopefully, we'll be busy. This place is make-or-break for me. My family think I'm mad coming all this way, but I needed to. I didn't want there to be any chance of me bumping into my ex with her new girlfriend."

Ah. "No, I get that." I swallowed the last of the tea. "Um, I was thinking. I wondered if you fancied a trip to the pictures or something one night. I thought you might get bored on your own in the pod of an evening."

"I can't remember the last time I went out to see a film and didn't stream it at home. Where would we have to go around here?"

"Richmond is our best bet. Maybe one-night next week. We could grab something to eat first if you want."

Chrissy took the mugs and rinsed them under the hot tap. "Sounds like fun. Can I let you know which day?"

"Sure. Of course. Whatever suits. Amy is fine by herself, and I can drive."

"Wonderful. Then it's a date."

Which it wasn't. Was it?

# 5. Chrissy

After a lot of hard work, by first thing Saturday morning, everything was ready. I sat sipping coffee with Claire at eight-thirty, attempting to still both our nerves. We had three clients booked in, but there was always a chance someone might turn up without checking in advance. I'd been through everything over and over with Claire. Her hands were shaking even now as they clasped the mug.

"I've watched loads of those wedding dress programmes online, and I've learnt the names of the different styles and accessories. I don't want to let you down."

"You won't" I assured her. I placed my hand on her arm. "Just remember every bride will be different. We may be the first place they've visited or the twentieth. A bride may have fixed ideas or no idea and be prepared to be led. I've had people come in with drawings they made as a child of what they want. Our first customer is due here at nine-thirty."

A knock on the door made us jump.

Claire stood first. "I'll get it." She hurried from the kitchen and returned a couple of minutes later with her arms full of flowers.

"Wow. It's a good job I thought of buying vases."

"I know. Aren't they amazing? You've three bunches with cards in each."

I stood and opened the cupboard to find the various flower receptacles. "Here," I said, placing them on the counter. "We can put them in these and position them in the showing arena." I filled each with water. "Let's see who they are from."

I picked out the cards from the flowers. The first two bunches were from my parents and Rob and Ingrid wishing me good luck. The last was from Beth and Amy. I had to admit I was surprised but pleased. We settled each bunch into a container.

"These are so lovely," Claire enthused.

"They are. And it was kind of Beth to send something."

"That's so like her," Claire explained. "She never forgets a birthday or anniversary. And these smell lovely. Let's hope we don't have clients who are allergic."

*Indeed.*

At nine-twenty, the sound of an engine alerted us someone had arrived. I sent Claire to the door to greet them and waited inside. I'd chosen a pale blue suit and white blouse today. I'd made the suit myself. My long hair was fashioned into a loose bun. I aimed to look business-like and efficient but softened by the colour and hair-style. I was conscious of my accent being southern among these northerners. The door opened and Claire led in three women —at my guess, mother of the bride and chief bridesmaid/best friend. I could spot the bride immediately. I stepped forward.

"Welcome to This is Me Brides. My name is Chrissy

Wychling and I'm here today to find you a dress. You must be April."

"I am. This is my mum, Angie and my best friend, Rachel. Please can you help me? We only have a month and I've been to so many shops."

"So many," her mother echoed.

"Please, sit, all of you. Would you like a drink?" Claire took their orders and hurried to the kitchen while I spent time listening to all three, getting a history and making a mental note of what had happened so far in this bride's journey to her dress.

"I mean, I know I'm big, but I refuse to compromise." Her glance at her mother told me there had been discussion over this. "Simon fell in love with me as I am. I want something elegant. I don't want a meringue or anything to fussy. My biggest issue is with my boobs. I don't want them on show, but I can't hide them either. I hate skin-tone net stuff, so none of that. What have you got?" Her folded arms suggested she expected me to stamp on her dreams just like other shops had done.

I took out a folder of basic dress designs I'd drawn over the years covering all shapes and designs. It was a bit like one of those books where you could fold pages to get different tops halves on different bottoms. Claire made notes as we talked.

Once we'd finished, I was clear in my mind what she wanted and what she didn't. "Okay. I think I have an idea. Why don't you come to the changing area with us, April and we'll pick a few out from the racks. Remember, each dress can be altered, as necessary."

April gave one nervous glance back and followed us. I took out a plain dress from the rail with a corseted top which would control her top half, V-necked lace which covered her shoulders and long sleeves with mother of pearl buttons. A tiny belt covered in similar decorations would emphasise her waist. I stood behind her pulling in the ties at the back while she told me about her husband-to-be.

"Can I have a veil?" she asked, while I tied the laces in the familiar intricate pattern I'd learned years ago. "Maybe something in the same lace. Could I get a band to match this one around my waist. Is that possible?"

"If you want it, it's possible," I assured her.

"My hair will be up on the day. I'll need shoes as well. I wonder if I could get pearls stuck on them."

"We have a pair of simple satin shoes, not too high, which would suit," Claire said. "I'd say you're a size seven."

"How did you know?"

"I've worked in shoe sales," Claire explained.

I finished tying up the back. I'd covered the mirror in here. "Would you like to see before we go in?"

"No, let's do it like they do on the TV. I want the surprise." She held out her arms. "I love how the sleeves hook over my finger at the end."

"I'll pop next door and get your mum and friend to close their eyes," Claire said. She sounded more excited than the bride.

"Are you ready?" I asked fingers crossed.

I led her into the main room and onto the small podium for the reveal. Everyone loved the drama of it all—even me. I knew the moment I saw her reflection in the mirrors that I'd made the right choice.

"Okay, everyone. Open your eyes."

The gasps then smiles told me they agreed. April swayed from side to side. "It even has pockets," she said.

"That dress is stunning," her friend said. "You were right about not going strapless. It shows off your figure perfectly."

"Mum?" I asked.

She wiped away a tear. "It's perfect. It's you. You never did like fuss or clutter. Your house has simple lines and so does this."

"And it fits, Mum. It fits first time. I don't need it altered." She turned to me. "That's right, isn't it? And it's within our price range, Mum."

"It most certainly is. We can pack the dress for you today or you can collect it and the shoes and headband nearer the day. Whatever you want. Now, we'd better get the dress removed and put to one side for you."

When they'd left, Claire hugged me. "That was amazing."

"It's not always so easy. I think she'd been trying to make her mother happy not herself."

The second bride proved less easy to please and we didn't make a sale—yet. She had time and we were the first place she'd been to. I had hopes she'd return. We had a couple of drop-ins during the afternoon. I showed them a few designs and they booked appointments to return. At three, Carrie arrived with her mother and three aunties in tow. I settled them ready to talk.

"She's too big for everything, aren't you, darling?" As soon as her mother spoke, my hackles rose. I remembered my sister-in-law's grandmother and every other bride facing the same criticism. Carrie nodded. I glanced at one aunt who grimaced. There was my ally.

"Not in this bridal shop," I said, making eye contact with them all. "Please, tell me what you want."

"She needs something simple that covers everywhere—you

know all the overhanging bits—and we're not made of money. We know what you lot can be like adding on little extras."

I took a deep breath. "Claire, could you get drinks for the ladies while Carrie and I go into the back and have a chat about dresses." I needed to get her away.

In the storage area, she sank onto a chair. "I'm sorry about my mother."

I pulled the other chair next to her. "It's all right. I've met lots of mothers and lots of brides. Do you want plain and simple?"

She shook her head. "No. Usually, I try to hide myself, but this is my day. Much to everyone's astonishment, I've found this great bloke who loves me, and I love him. Everyone will be staring at me anyway, so I want to give them something to look at My mum always says who's going to look at you when I worry about clothes, but everyone does when you're my size. People stare and make comments—people I don't know feel they have a right to judge. She had me on diets when I was still in school. After university, I moved to Glasgow, got away from her, and met Phil, but the wedding is will be here and I'm back home again attempting to have some control. Even though I have a partner now, Mum's not happy. She thinks he encourages me not to try."

"Sometimes, we have to accept we can't always be who our parents would like us to be. And this is *your* day."

"Sometimes, you wouldn't think so. At work, I'm in charge of a team of twenty people, and I love it. I'm determined to invite *my* friends and have *my* wedding."

*Good for you.* "Well," I said taking her hand. "Let's find the perfect dress for you with all the bling you could ever want."

After a couple of tries, we found what Carrie wanted. The

dress itself was simple, but the rhinestones made it shimmer and it had enough netting to make it stand out over her hips. The train was long—I'd added a piece with more stones, along with net on the arms and two straps encrusted with crystals and a belt. The corsetry gave her more shape.

"I want to see before we go back in there," she said.

I unveiled the mirror and she gasped, then cried.

"I'm sorry. These are happy tears. I love how it shimmers in the light."

Claire entered the room. "Oh wow. You look incredible. Your audience is getting restless."

"I never thought—"

I placed my arms on Carrie's shoulders. "Claire's right. You are stunning." I grabbed a tiara and veil and secured them to her hair. "There."

"On the day. Can you come? Please say you can. It's in Bedale two months from now."

I'd done weddings before. "Let me know the date and I'll be there. Now. Let's go out there and wow them."

Before the mother could speak, the aunties were on their feet. Each hugged Claire and in my head I thanked them.

"Mum? What do you think?"

"It's quite fussy, but it suits you." Not quite praise, but near enough for now.

"Chrissy says she'll come to the wedding to make sure it's perfect on the day."

"It's all right," I said. We'll just help with the dress. We don't expect to be guests."

"Are you sure, Claire?"

"Yes, Mum. As the shop says—this dress is me."

Later, Claire handed me a coffee. "Is it always like this?" she asked. "Will I always want to throttle the mothers. I'm so glad mine isn't like those two, especially the second one. I feel like I should take a counselling course. Thank goodness for the aunties. There's an awful lot of baggage in that family."

I sipped the coffee. "You'd better get used to it. I've seen much worse. And if you're serious, a course would be useful. When I did my degree we learned it wasn't so much about the clothes as the people who would wear them. Everyone has hang-ups about their bodies and weddings are the occasions to reveal them. Mothers of the bride feel those pressures too. You have two families coming together."

"You sound like you're speaking from experience."

I sighed. "I am. There were two brides at my wedding after all. I avoided dress problems by not wearing a dress and not everyone approved."

"I didn't know weddings were such a minefield. I've a lot to learn, and not only about frocks. Any plans for tonight?"

"Nope," I said. "Do the paperwork, lie on my bed, and stare at the TV. Another glamorous Saturday night. Still, I'm off to the pictures at Richmond with Beth on Wednesday."

"Good. You should get out and discover the area. We've so many beautiful places. And Beth knows this area so well. *She* could do with getting out more. Farms keep you busy."

"I suppose they do—all those early mornings. Thanks for today. There's nothing like jumping in both feet first."

She smiled at me. "Maybe, but I think I'm going to love it."

# 6. Deth

I didn't get much chance to show Chrissy the landscape as we travelled along country roads to Richmond. Dusk came too early for views, and I needed my headlights switched on. It had been ages since I'd been anywhere other than into Netherington to the White Hart after dark. I made a mental note to at least show Chrissy around the farm and show her the landscape of the Dales. I had no idea what Kent was like.

"Is here different to where you grew up?" I asked, to make conversation.

"Kent's odd," Chrissy answered. "It's rural, and yet it was a big mining area. It has the coast, of course, and used to be famous for seafood like oysters—I don't appreciate them myself —it's like eating snot. Oysters were sent to London and even poorer people could afford to eat them. Pockets of the county are so deprived and yet house prices can be ridiculous. It's a place of real contrasts. For some reason, I've never felt any real affinity with the place. Then again, I did live in London for three years."

"We could have been there around the same time. I went to

university in the city, met my ex-husband, got into a fantastic law practice, fell pregnant, had Amy, then went back to work. Life in London was nothing like here—so many people and always so busy."

"But you chose to come back here."

"I did." I didn't want to explain—not now. "And you made the same decision."

"My family still think I'm mad upping sticks to somewhere I know nothing about—you were coming home. But I did my research. So far, I've had customers come from places as far away as Leeds and Whitby and our appointments calendar is growing. My brother did a great job with the website. He's also arranged for an interview with one of the biggest bridal magazines, and on Saturday next, we're off to a big bridal fayre in York. Claire has been a godsend, by the way. She's great with the customers and keen to learn."

"So the business has taken off quickly, then?"

"It's ticking over. I need to keep a close eye on the accounts. The dresses vary in price, but we charge for a personal service and appointments. I need to find an accountant. My old one still works for my ex."

"Ah."

"Ah, indeed. Still, the divorce settlement is sorted now, and I've decided business and pleasure don't go together, at least not permanently."

We entered Richmond and I headed for the parking area in the centre. "The pub is over there," I said once I'd found a space.

"It looks old."

I nodded. "It's an eighteenth-century coaching house, not as ancient as the White Hart, but It's been modernised inside.

People come to stay in the town to see the local landmarks, like the castle. It depends if you're into history. There's plenty to see and do around here."

Chrissy chuckled. "I'm from Kent. We have history. I've been on school trips to most places, and seen the spot where Thomas Becket was killed more than a few times—you know they put more blood down for the tourists. I was always more about the fashions than the buildings, though. Sometimes, a ruin is a ruin, and another castle is another castle. I've always been more interested in the people who live in them."

"I do like a castle though. Some of them appear so romantic in the stories, but I bet they were freezing." I opened the car door and stepped out. Chrissy got out the other side. "You should meet Jed's husband," I said over the roof of the car. "His speciality is the Dark Ages. He'd show you how a Viking dressed and tell you about how they lived. Jorvik is worth a visit."

"I'll add it to my list. I'd like to go to the seaside. I do miss the coast. I'm trying to decide between Scarborough, Bridlington, or going further to Whitby for the Dracula connection."

Once in the bar, we were shown to our table and given menus. "We have an hour before the film begins," I explained. "Main courses only, then. We can buy sweets in the cinema or ice creams." I took off my coat.

"Wow. Your dress is something."

Chrissy stared and heat rushed into my face. I sat on the bench seat tucking myself under the table. Suddenly, I felt exposed even though I was fully covered. Chrissy took the seat opposite.

"Sorry. But I've only seen you in dungarees and wellies. That dress suits your figure. I have to admit, I'm envious."

I couldn't remember anyone ever telling me they were envious of my figure before. Yes, I went in and out in all the right places, but too far out and not enough in. "There's this place online which sells these quirky frocks. I like the style and it's nice to get an opportunity to wear something different from dungarees and have proper shoes on my feet. Do you always wear suits?"

Chrissy was dressed in brown striped trousers and waistcoat with a pale blue shirt. Her blonde hair was tied back. She grinned. I guessed I wasn't the first to ask.

"I like suits because they suit me." She chuckled. "I'd love to be able to wear a dress like yours, but it would hang off me. I envy your curves. I have these wide shoulders and long arms and legs, and barely any shape to speak of. In university, I was popular with other students because I was the perfect model. Clothes hung from me. I have this metabolism thing. It's superfast. My dad has it too. We can eat anything and not put on weight. But it also means I have to be more careful to eat the right food and not live on chocolate and cake. People think we're lucky. As a kid I was so gawky, like a baby giraffe. Other girls at school developed shapes. I used to pad my bras and hips sometimes."

"It's daft, isn't it? You wanted curves and I hated mine. Why are we so rarely happy with what we've got?" She stared at me, and shivers ran up my spine.

"I'm not selling myself, am I?"

"It's okay. I'm not shopping." I had no idea why I said that. "Sorry, that was rude."

"Don't worry. But you should be happy with yourself. You're beautiful. especially with your hair down. It's such a glorious deep colour and so shiny."

I dragged my gaze away. I wasn't used to such compliments. I stared at the table and fiddled with the cutlery until the heat in my face subsided. I lifted my gaze to find her waiting. "Such dark hair runs in the family," I said, desperate to change the subject. "And Netherings have lived around here for centuries. Maybe we descend from the original Celts. Anyway, what do you fancy to eat? I can recommend the pork in cider. I know the farm where the meat comes from. The pigs are free-range."

Chrissy glanced at me.

"Sorry. You're not a vegetarian, are you?"

"No. I suppose I'm being a typical townie. Except for wanting better-quality food, I don't I think of where it's from. I'm not sure I could do what you do. I know that's bad of me."

I took a deep breath. "When I was young, I hated seeing the animals being taken for slaughter. My dad was a stickler for animal welfare, even though it cut into his profits. But still, the cattle and lambs were taken. Farming is a business. We provide food for people who don't want to have to think about how it gets on their plate." I didn't want to argue, but at some point I seemed to have this conversation with everyone I met. I hated defending what I did, but death was a reality of life.

Chrissy reached out her hand and touched mine.

"I'm sorry. And the pork sounds wonderful." I nodded at the hovering waiter who took our order.

"No, I'm sorry. I sometimes get defensive." I didn't move my hand and neither did she. "Maybe we should talk about something else. What about your surname? Wychling is interesting." A slight smile crossed her face, and I relaxed a little.

"There aren't many of us, and it's usually traced back to Kent. Apparently, back in Medieval times a Baron Wychling owned a lot of land. Younger sons probably sowed their oats on the wrong side of the blanket, and I suspect my family descend from them—there's certainly no money or land. There were rumours about the Wychlings of old casting spells to get their wealth—hence the name. Wychling women were even burnt at the stake when Matthew Hopkins, the Witchfinder General, was roaming the land in the seventeenth century."

"Sounds fascinating. There's a story of a big cat who roams the villages and fields at night around here—you know sheep being found half eaten. It's more likely careless tourists letting their dogs off the lead, but people like to tell tales."

The food arrived. We ate quickly, conscious time was moving on and we didn't want to be late for the film. Chrissy asked about the farm and what we produced—I could talk about my world till the cows came home.

"I've never had sheep's cheese or yoghurt," Chrissy said.

"I'll bring you some."

"And you have different breeds of sheep and highland cows?"

"For the tourists," I explained. "My dad used to like raising rare breeds. We have cute ones like the Valois for the visitors. I'll give you a tour of the farm."

"I'd like that."

I glanced at my watch. "We'd better pay and get going."

The film was good, but I was yawning by the time it finished. On the journey home, we talked about the movie and kept the conversation light. I parked next to the glamping pods. The other two were also occupied and light shone from their windows. Chrissy stepped out and I wound the window down.

She leaned on the roof. "Thank you. This was fun. Next time let me take you somewhere. We could have a day at the coast if you can spare the time."

I yawned again. "Sorry, this is late for me. I'm up at six in the morning."

Chrissy nodded. "I've nothing booked in for tomorrow, but we never know if someone will arrive. We've people on Friday and Saturday, then Sunday we're at a wedding fayre."

"You should try the hot tub to relax," I said.

"Maybe you could join me. Everyone needs to relax." The sound of laughter floated on the breeze. "It sounds like your other visitors are enjoying the facilities." She stepped away from the car. "Don't work too hard. And the suggestion is there if you fancy it." She grinned and strolled off along the path leaving me more than a little curious of what might happen if I took her up on her offer.

# 7. Deth

It had been a long, but successful day. The excitement of Amy winning the Yorkshire young dog handler competition at least meant she would be happy. I'd dropped her off at her friend's house and brought Ralph home.

"Okay, chooks, that's all of you safe for the night."

Ned had seen a fox hanging around the previous day, so I double-checked everything. Ralph trotted alongside me. He'd put up with me and Ned, but he missed his human, especially after they'd been the centre of attention for much of the day. The sound of music playing came from the nearest of the pods when I reached the back door. I put Ralph in the kitchen and waited for him settle into his box next to the Aga. He would no doubt be snoring in minutes after such a busy day. Boredom and curiosity got the better of me, so I wandered down the path to the glamping pods knowing the only customer I had tonight was Chrissy. The gravel crunched under my feet and the stars twinkled in the dark sky. There were hopes we might even see the Aurora Borealis this far south over the weekend. I'd seen it before, but every time was special.

I didn't want to surprise Chrissy so shouted out my presence. "Hello, it's Beth."

"I'm back here. Come round. It's a lovely night. I wasn't expecting visitors. I'm in the hot tub."

Each of our pods had a tub at the back, which gave them privacy and a view over the fields to watch the sun setting. At this time of the year, it had already disappeared over the horizon, leaving the outside in pitch darkness. Chrissy must have been made of strong stuff as there was a nip in the air, though the water was heated. I reached the opening and stepped onto the wooden platform. Chrissy lay with her head resting on a cushion and a glass of what looked like champagne in her hand. She was naked from what I could tell with the top of her shoulders sticking out of the bubbling water. Steam filled the air. Heat rushed into my cheeks as I blushed. I decided to brazen it out.

"I'm sorry. I didn't realise." *That you were stark naked.* "I heard the music. Genesis is an unusual choice." I stood moving from foot to foot, unsure what to do. Chrissy didn't appear to be even slightly bothered.

"I was brought up with it. Dad loves them. I find they absorb my thoughts while I drift along with the words and music. Why don't you join me? There's more drink in the kitchen, and there's plenty of room in here."

I glanced around. I'm not sure who I was expecting to see. We were the only people on this part of the farm. "Umm, I don't have a costume or anything."

Chrissy grinned. "Neither do I. If I close my eyes you can slip in, though I don't know why you're worried."

"Sorry," I replied, confused.

"With those curves and your beautiful hair, I bet you get all sorts of admirers."

*Not so you'd notice.*

"Come on. Get in. It'll be nice to have company."

"All right. Why not." I stripped to my underwear, but left my knickers on, climbed the step then slipped into the warm water until I was covered to my neck. Chrissy opened her eyes and smiled. She passed me the glass.

"Here. Have a sip of this. It's the good stuff."

I took a sip as suggested. She was right. The last time I'd tasted fizzy stuff of this quality had been when I'd helped seal a deal for a big company in London. Inevitably, the bubbles went up my nose. I handed the glass back and placed my arms over my breasts. Was I imagining them trying to bob to the surface? Chrissy stared right at me.

"You honestly don't have anything to worry about, you know. I envy those curves of yours. I can see they're there even under those dungarees you wear all the time. I've a trained eye. I could pull a dress from a rail and know I'd picked the perfect one for you. Whereas me, like I said, I'm all arms and legs with swimmer's shoulders and disappointing boobs. I love women who go in and out in all the right places.."

It wasn't just the heat of the water making my face turn red. I'd never been comfortable in my own skin. In school, I'd hated the communal showers. All those girls worrying about what they looked like—every blemish, every spot, every freckle, and every inch of fat. I found Chrissy's compliments difficult to accept even now, but maybe it was the champagne, or maybe it was that we were both practically naked, somehow I summoned up the courage from somewhere to ask a question.

"Are you flirting with me?"

Chrissy stretched her arms out either side of her along the edge of the tub. "Would it be a problem if I was?"

I considered the idea for a moment. "I don't know. It's been a while since anyone bothered. I don't get out much. The farm keeps me busy and as you know, I don't get to dress up often, except when I go to the White Hart, and even them I don't usually bother. I'm thirty-nine and three-quarters and have a seventeen-year-old daughter. All I'm expecting now is arthritis to set in and my gall bladder to go. What do they say? Fair, fat, and forty? That's two out of three for me."

Chrissy scowled. "Stop it. You're beautiful, as I tell every woman who comes through my door afraid they won't find a dress to fit them for their big day."

"Now I *know* you're flirting with me. Look, I don't want to lead you on. I'm not gay. I was married to a man." *Why the hell did I say that? I'm making all sorts of presumptions.*

She sat up and smiled at me. "What does that matter? Who doesn't love being reminded they're beautiful, whatever their sexuality? Admit it, me flirting with you has made you feel noticed—just a little bit." She held up her hand with her finger and thumb a fraction apart.

*She isn't wrong.*

I gave in and laughed at my stupidity. "Okay, you win. It has. Anyway, changing the subject. Is there a reason why you're out here in the hot tub drinking this champagne, listening to Genesis, and staring at the stars?"

"As it happens, there are reasons. Today, I sold a four-thousand-pound dress to a woman. The profit will pay Claire's wages for the month."

"Wow, I can't imagine spending so much on an outfit." I

thought of all the things I could buy for the farm with that sort of spare money.

"Phenella Mountjoy could afford it. Lovely woman who listened to advice."

"Phen was here today? I've known her for years. She's getting married next June to such a nice bloke who adores her."

"She said she'd searched everywhere for the right dress until today when I put it together for her. You know her then?"

"I do. Her family have an estate locally. She's actually Lady Phenella Mountjoy. Her father is an earl."

"Shit. I should have called her mother Countess of somewhere. She didn't say."

I smiled. "Phen wouldn't. She's down to earth and doesn't stand on ceremony. And the countess is the daughter of a fishmonger from Whitby. She hands out all the prizes at the local shows. My mum used to win best cake every year. Anyway, you said reasons."

"Yep. The other reason is it's my thirty-fifth birthday today."

"Well, happy birthday to you."

"Thank you." She gazed at me again. "It's the first birthday I've spent by myself. I wasn't even born on my own. I have a twin brother. Rob was born fifteen minutes after me."

"It must be strange, being apart." Tears welled up inside me, but I pushed away the memory. Now was not the time.

"It is. I spoke to him and my parents earlier, but it's different from being there in person."

I decided to change the subject. "Things seem to be going well with the bridal shop. I've seen a regular stream of cars parked. And if Phen has bought a dress from you, you can be sure her friends will follow."

"That's good to know. She said something about a feature in *Yorkshire Life*. People get to here by word of mouth as well as checking out our website. Over the years, I've discovered each bride is different. Many buy their dresses a year in advance, while others wait until the last moment. The key is knowing what to stock. I try to keep dresses that are easily adapted up to size forty, and I can do bigger. I don't want any bride to go away without a dress. I can add sleeves or even whole lace bodices, skirts, and trains. I've corsets which go over a dress or lingerie sets to go under. I've plain, and lace, and beaded, and even dresses in red, black, or purple. I've sleek dresses, those with fishtails, simple A- line frocks, those which hug a figure, those which create one, and those that cover a bride from head to toe. I'm a trained tailor and can alter anything on a bought dress."

"Sounds like farming in a way. I have to be able to turn my hand to anything, though I'm no good at fixing our rather unreliable tractor. You must have to be a counsellor sometimes as well."

I thought back to the dress I'd worn at my wedding and the arguments between me and my mother. The woman selling the dress had been a saint. "I expect there are many heated discussions, especially if family and friends are involved."

"So many. But I've learned when to speak and when to stay silent. I have to say Claire is a real find. She's brilliant with the brides and their families, and she's got a great memory for stock and what will suit."

"Karen says she's loving it. You'll get a free meal at the White Hart whenever you want. Claire's last boss was a pain. She's much happier now." I yawned. The warmth and activity of the day was clearly catching up with me. "And I think I'd better be going."

"I expect you're up early in the morning. There's no lie- in for farmers."

"No. The sheep are milked every day, and the lambs need looking after. The other stock needs extra feed until the grass starts growing. Then there are the chickens and ducks. Amy has her horse. Jed wants us to get pygmy goats. Apparently yoga with goats is a thing. I mean—who knew? Still, at least this winter has been mild compared to last year when we had snow."

"I thought this was lambing season now heading into spring."

"It is for some. We milk producers have a system." I didn't want to explain how we rotated so we'd always have milk for sale. Um, I need to get out if you don't mind. I'll throw my dungarees on with my coat and wellies."

"Help yourself."

She didn't turn away. *Screw it. She could stare if she wanted to. Sometimes, it felt good to be admired.* Once out of the water the cold air hit me, my nipples stiffened, and I dressed quickly.

"We must do this again," Chrissy said. "It's good to have someone to chat to of an evening."

Guilt hit me. I hadn't thought of inviting her to eat with us. Why hadn't I? It wasn't like me. "You must come to us for dinner one night and meet Amy properly. I'm not much of a cook, but I can throw something together."

She stared up at me with those big blue eyes. Her lashes were long, and she had well-defined cheekbones, especially when she smiled, which she was now.

"Maybe I could help you. I love to cook."

"Then we'll have to sort something." I shivered.

"Wow," Chrissy said suddenly. "Where did those streaks of colour come from?" I turned back to see lights flashing across the sky—greens, reds, yellows. They danced in patterns across the northern sky. The sight was mesmerising.

"It's the Northern Lights," I said. "They said we might be able to see them tonight. It doesn't happen often this far south."

Chrissy stared. "It's so beautiful. I've seen pictures and videos, but this is spectacular."

I shivered again. "I'll leave you to watch. Sometimes it's like you can hear them too. I need to get back to my warm house. It's been nice. I'll sort out a meal next week."

"I'd like that." Her eyes didn't leave the sky when I walked away. Ten minutes later, I was back in the house. It always seemed extra quiet when Amy was away. I checked the Aga and gave Ralph a few extra treats. knowing he might follow me upstairs if his person wasn't about.

In the bathroom, I stood cleaning my teeth and examined my face in the mirror. Okay, I had the family nose—long and straight, but in proportion to the rest of my features. My mouth was full-lipped. I had dimples when I smiled. My eyes were clear and dark. The lines only appeared if I smiled or frowned. I thought I appeared younger than my age. However, I wasn't used to someone flirting with me, or my complementing figure, but Chrissy had seemed genuine. And I had to admit it was nice to be appreciated rather than told I'd be so much more attractive if I lost a few pounds. I wondered idly what it would be like to be able to eat anything. I'd given up diets long ago. Working on a farm gave me more than enough exercise, tramping around fields and lifting bales of hay, holding on to sheep as they gave birth or were sheared. As a mother, I'd been determined not to give my daughter any hang-ups about her size or appearance.

I padded across the landing to my bedroom, undressed, rubbed cream into my face, and slipped into my pyjamas—brushed cotton and not at all sexy, being covered with penguins. Lying in bed, I stared at the ceiling then reached over to the top drawer and grabbed my little friend. *Why not?* An orgasm would help me sleep.

I slipped the bullet vibrator between my legs and found the right spot. I didn't use anything fancy. My little friend worked for me—hands-free if I tightened my thighs around it. I reeled though my usual fantasies. What would it be tonight? Sometimes, I involved myself and sometimes I was simply a voyeur. I wasn't one for porn—too much artificial screaming for my taste. Anyway, I'd found my imagination could produce better.

*What if I'd let the flirting go further?* The question slipped into my mind. I hadn't yet switched on the vibrator—I had to time these things, or I'd come before I'd finished the fantasy.

I'd had few lovers at university, then I'd met Graham, and that was that. There's been no one else. In my fantasies, I'd only thought of men, but what if the person was female? A woman would know my body as she knew her own. She'd know what to touch, how to touch, what pressure to use. I pressed the switch. Sex with a woman wouldn't be the same. I imagined fingers caressing me and moved my hand to my breast to rub my nipple. My body writhed at this sensation along with the delightful tingle between my thighs. I imagined kisses all over my body leading to my clit. Graham had never licked me there —used fingers, yes, but not tongue. I wriggled, reached down, and pressed the vibrator against my clit, trying to imagine what a tongue would feel like—what Chrissy's tongue might feel like. *No—mustn't go there.*

I trawled my stories. What if I was the head of the household, this time not seduced by the footman but by my lady's maid. I let myself imagine her taking off my clothes with accidental caresses, me sighing, her saying she knew what I needed—my *Bridgerton* fantasy with a new twist—all those petticoats to lift and no knickers. The tingles on my clit increased. I raised my hips, chasing satisfaction. The imaginary maid spread my legs and smiled at me.

"I know what you need , mistress."

She buried her face between my thighs. I felt myself opening up. My orgasm came from deep within and burst out. I gasped then instinctively put my hand in my mouth so as not to make a sound. I let the waves of pleasure wash over me until I could stand them no more, removed the bullet, and let my breath slow before rolling over and tucking my duvet around me.

*Is this what I want?* The question shocked me, and I opened my eyes. The bedroom door creaked open, Ralph entered and jumped on the bed to settle at the end. *Don't be silly.* I gave myself a telling-off. *It's just another fantasy. It's not real.* But maybe it did tell me one thing—I needed to get laid.

# 8. Chrissy

"Are you okay? You've been quiet this morning. I was expecting a million instructions."

I followed the satnav's direction to take the third turning off the roundabout. I'd hired a van to carry the rails and selection of dresses and was unfamiliar with the voice as well as the route. "I'm sorry. My mind is a bit occupied. Do you have any questions?" I caught Claire glancing at me out of the corner of my eye.

"Nothing really. I guess it's like being in the shop."

"Porters will help us to unload and set up. I've packed curtains to make a changing room if needed and as many rails as possible. There'll be lots of people like us there. Some brides attend fayres to browse and others go determined to find their dress along with everything else. The fayre will have everything you could need from dresses, to catering, cakes, and acts for the party afterwards."

"I keep imagining it's like the episode from *Gavin and Stacey*. I'm hoping there's a chocolate fountain giving away samples."

I grinned. I knew the episode she meant. Real life wasn't so different. "Remember, we have a niche audience, though there may be others who sell larger sizes, this is our speciality, our unique selling point. If brides aren't certain, we make appointments for them to visit the shop. Whole families tend to come to these places, so remember to keep an eye on what the entourage want as well. Someone always has the power, and we want to make sure it's the bride. *This is Me* isn't merely the name of our company, it's the message we want our brides to exude no matter what. Their happiness is our priority." I paused. "Bloody hell. I'm coming out with more platitudes than Polonius in *Hamlet*."

"I did *Hamlet* for A-level. I couldn't believe Shakespeare invented all those sayings."

"We did it too. I wasn't a fan."

I took the next left and we rolled up in front of the venue— a large country house hotel. We were directed to the back of the building, which gave direct access to the room where we'd been told to set up. An hour later, we were ready for our first wedding fayre in the county. It would be a long day. I shifted thoughts of last night out of my mind. I needed to focus. The door opened at ten-thirty and the mayhem began.

After an hour of people walking past us, I began to panic, then a woman stood gazing at our sign. Her friend pushed her towards us.

"Go on. You don't have to buy anything."

"But what if they don't have a dress that will fit. I couldn't bear it again." From where I stood, I could see the tears forming. Claire beat me and rose from her seat. I watched my protégé go into action. This girl didn't appear to be much older than her.

"Hi, my name is Claire. Why don't you come in and see what we have."

Her friend spoke first. "It says you can find a dress for any bride. Well, Nat is on a budget, and let's say she's had some bad experiences. I saw your site online and dragged her here."

"Why don't you search through our dresses on the rails, pick anything you like, then we'll see what we can do. We have all sorts of payment plans, and we can rent out certain dresses." I stood as she guided the bride in my direction.

"Natalie, is it?" She nodded. "Well, Natalie, why don't we discuss what sort of dress you want. There is no size or shape we can't cater for." I was gratified to see the start of a smile forming.

"Really?"

"Really."

The third dress was the right one. She cried. Her friend cried. I had tears. The shape was simple. The skirt spread around her. The bodice gave her a waist. The sleeves covered the top of her arms. It was basic, but beautiful. I pulled out a veil and placed the comb into her hair.

"There. The crowning glory."

"Can I send a photograph to my mum. She couldn't come. She's got flu."

"Of course." Behind me another couple wandered in and headed for the rack of dresses. I nodded to Claire who hurried over. Natalie hugged me and her friend hugged me. These were the moments I loved. I boxed the dress up. It would need a few alterations to secure the changes we'd made.

"You can collect it in two weeks," I said. "Payment on collection."

Then the mayhem did begin. We sold two other dresses

needing no changes and made four appointments before lunch. We allowed ourselves thirty minutes to eat our sandwiches.

"I spoke to Beth last night," I said casually. "She told me our customer from yesterday is, in fact, *Lady* Phenella Mountjoy."

"I know. I mentioned her name to Mum last night. She went to school with Aunty Beth and Mum. Selling her a dress could help us. I bet there'll be loads of posh folk at the wedding. It could even be in a magazine."

I loved how Claire was fully invested after a few weeks working with me and used *"us"* so often. That was what I needed in an assistant. "You're right. So much of this game is word of mouth recommendations. I want to give people their best day, but it doesn't do us any harm if we make money along the way."

I paused for a moment to consider my next words. "It's a hard life, farming. I'm surprised Beth returned from living in London."

"Mum was too. But there are some family obligations you just can't ignore, aren't there? Netherings have farmed this land for hundreds of years. Beth could have employed a manager, but it wouldn't have been the same. Ties to the land are strong around here. My mum's family were blacksmiths in the past— generations of them. If you find a family, you'll often find they were shepherds, or coopers, or wheelwrights, or miners. Occupations ran in families. I expect they did in your family."

*She's skilfully moved the conversation around.* "We had miners too, and fishermen, as well as those who sold oysters from Whitstable. Others were hop growers." I paused again, but Claire munched on her sandwich and didn't fill the silence.

"I suppose living and working in London isn't all it's

cracked up to be, especially if your marriage is falling apart." I kept digging.

"I wouldn't know. I was ten when Beth came back. Marriages fail for all sorts of reasons. You were married, weren't you?"

*Damn, I walked into that one.* "I was." I didn't want to talk about it. This conversation was getting me nowhere. I bagged the rubbish. "We'd better get back. Dresses don't sell themselves."

The afternoon was busy. We didn't sell much except to someone who had a week to find a dress. Her whole family hugged us. Others made appointments to come to the shop after giving me ideas of what they were looking for. It meant I could search for dresses myself. Minutes before we thought the event was over, a customer wheeled herself in with her dog at her side, and a person behind her.

"I need a dress."

Her voice cracked. Her companion squeezed her shoulders, and the dog rested its head on her knee.

"Come on, sis. Just because..." Her brother paused and stared at us. The dog lay next to the chair—there if needed.

"My name is Chrissy," I said. "And this is my assistant, Claire. How can we help?"

She wiped away a tear. "I'm sorry. It's been a long day. My name is Izzy, and this is my brother, James. I'm getting married in three months to the most wonderful man. I've been trying to find a dress in my size, and which will work with my wheelchair, for what seems like forever."

"Okay," I said. "I'll be honest and say, we haven't got anything on the rails here, but let me sit with you and discuss what you need. I'll make a few sketches and you can make an appointment to visit our shop."

"Is it accessible? So many have steps or narrow doors."

Claire moved closer. "Totally. There are no steps or thresholds at the doors which are wide enough for larger chairs, and the whole building gives wheelchair access including the facilities. We have a transfer board if you want to move to different seating."

Izzy smiled and glanced up at her brother. "And I can bring my dog?"

"Of course. We know how well-trained support dogs are and he'll be kept on a lead. Our premises is on a farm. Now, let me get my sketch pad and we'll work on some ideas."

Izzy's smile filled my heart with joy. These were the moments I lived for. After thirty minutes, I had several ideas and we'd made an appointment for Izzy to visit. As I watched her and James leave, I thought it had been a good day.

It took time to pack everything away even with the porters' help. At the shop, Claire helped me unpack though we didn't put everything back on the racks.

"Mum's coming to pick me up," Claire said. "Thank you for today. I learnt so much watching you work. I also had chance to wander round the venue and left a few cards for the inn. Mum and Dad do weddings, and any publicity seldom hurts. Can I see the sketches you did for Izzy?"

We sat in the viewing area, and I took out my pad.

"So, the dress can't be too big and wide because of the wheels, and the same with the sleeves."

I nodded. "The last thing a bride needs on her big day, is to get her dress ripped. The top half needs room so she can move her arms, so it can't be too tight. But a bride still wants something beautiful not utilitarian. In this case, I can make a simple dress, but create a lace bodice and skirt to overlay with the purple floral motif for drama. I worked with wheelchair users for my designs at university."

The front door opened. "In here, Mum," Claire called out.

Karen pushed through the swing doors carrying a large paper bag with a handle. My nose detected something that smelled good.

"I brought you a couple of portions of tonight's special," she said. "I expect you haven't eaten much. Good day?"

Claire stood. "It was brilliant, Mum. I'm learning such a lot. I'll tell you in the car."

"You get yourself in there, then. You look dead on your feet." Karen waited until Claire left.

"She has Wednesday off this week, and she's getting double pay for today," I said, knowing from Karen's expression of concern she was worried I was exploiting her daughter. "And I couldn't ask for a better assistant. She's such a quick learner and great with customers. Finding Claire has made the start of this journey so much easier."

Karen's tense shoulders relaxed. "She sings your praises all the time. We're grateful, you know. She had no idea what she wanted to do, but I think she's found her niche with you. I know I have no reason to worry, but I'm a parent and it goes with the territory. Anyway, this food is to say thank you. George insisted you try his Beef Bourguignon served with rice. I know it's not easy to cook in those pods. It won't be easy to find a place to live around here either. So many properties are holiday homes now."

"I'll keep searching," I said. "And thank you for this. I am starving. It's been a long but successful day."

Karen grinned. "You're welcome to the food. I'll leave you to your evening. Please feel free to come and have dinner at the White Hart any time you like—on the house. Perhaps you could persuade Beth to come with you. She needs to get out more."

I followed Karen to the outer door, switching off the lights, and setting the alarms as I did.

"Tell Claire I don't need her until ten-thirty tomorrow. I've got to take the van back and I'm not certain of when I'll return. We don't have anyone booked in until the afternoon."

"I will," Karen said. I waved as the car moved off into the lane then locked up and carried my meal along the narrow path to the pod. Perhaps I *could* ask Beth if she wanted to have dinner with me one night.

# 9. Death

I picked up the young lamb from the small pen next to the huge space where the rest of the growing lambs, now weaned, gambolled around. Building this place had cost a small fortune but it was a necessary part of the milking process. Even so, we kept lambs and ewes together for longer than other businesses by a careful system of each farmer altering the time of their lambing season and freezing some of the milk to ensure a constant supply for our buyers. Farming was full of such logistics.

"Now, little one. I'm sorry your mum can't do this, but three is too many for her. You and your little friend will have to bunk down in here for now until you are old enough to go out." I picked up the bottle of milk and settled myself and the first lamb onto the hay bale.

This one wasn't one of our British Milk Sheep lambs, but instead one of the interesting or rare breeds we had at the farm to entertain the tourists who stayed in the pods. They were also part of a small selection my father had bred over the years along with his beloved Highland cattle. This lamb and its companion were Valois Blacknose sheep, considered to be the cutest sheep in the world and popular with visitors.

The lamb sucked greedily.

"Nothing wrong with your appetite, that's for certain." As a child I'd fed lambs rejected by their mothers or too small to thrive outside. We'd even kept them in the kitchen next to the Aga. I loved the simple joy of the process.

"And yes, you are the cutest thing I ever did see."

"Found you. Ned said you were in here. The taxi dropped me off from the station. Next time I need a van, I need to work out a better system."

I turned to see Beth strolling towards me. "I'd offer you ours, but I don't think you want to turn up at a wedding fayre with dresses smelling of sheep." I put the lamb down and picked up the other one.

Chrissy placed her coat on another bale and sat. "This lamb may be the most gorgeous animal I've ever seen. I know their breed has been on *Countryfile*."

"They have," I said. "My dad bred them along with Herdwicks, which aren't so pretty. These two need to be hand-fed."

Chrissy leaned over. "Could I have a go? I've never fed a lamb. To be honest, I've never fed anything—not even a baby."

"Sure. Make sure you keep the bottle at an angle but not too much. This one is eager to drink." I handed the lamb over and studied Chrissy as it fed successfully. Her eyes lit up and joy shone from her face as she gazed at the small creature she was feeding. I'd seen that so often before when tourists did the same. Somehow, this simple task softened peoples' expressions.

"She's keen," Chrissy said, struggling to hold the wriggling youngster.

"Luckily, they both are. Their mothers had triplets but can only feed two at a time, so we hand-feed them. In the past, we used to feed more. Now, we try to hand over the third lamb to a ewe who's had one. We've a good success rate."

"But the mothers aren't in with them now," Chrissy said gazing around the space.

I hated this conversation. "No, to get the milk, we separate them after six to eight weeks, like puppies and kittens are taken from their mothers. We leave them together longer than some. And those we keep eventually join the flock."

"And the rest go to market." Chrissy stared at the lamb then at me. "I know. I'm not stupid. I eat lamb. Here, it's more real, I suppose. I think she's finished."

I took the lamb from her and placed it back in the pen. "Anyway, you didn't come here to talk about lambs. How can I help? Is everything all right?"

"Yes, everything is fine. Claire and I had a good day at the fayre yesterday. Karen picked her up last night and suggested I come for dinner at the inn sometime this week. I wondered if you'd like to join me."

I sensed Karen's hand in this. She often asked me to visit, but she'd be busy, and I'd be sat there on my own. Sometimes, I went with Jed and Lars, but felt like a gooseberry, even on karaoke nights—Karen did love them so.

"Umm, when were you thinking?"

"Wednesday, maybe. If you have time. I know you're busy and you have to get up early. I can drive if you want a drink for a change."

"You do know this Wednesday is karaoke night. Karen has one a month."

Chrissy grinned at me. "That's all right. I love to sing."

Wednesday night, I fussed about what to wear. Maybe another dress? Chrissy had commented on how much that one had suited me. I rummaged in my wardrobe and picked out a cute dress in a fifties style I'd bought a few years back for a farmer's barn dance. It had elbow length sleeves, a round-necked bodice, a waistline which showed I had a figure, and a flared skirt. It was bright with blues and greens. I rooted through the mess of footwear at the bottom of the wardrobe for the Mary-Janes I'd bought to dance in. In front of the mirror, I swung the dress to and fro.

"That's nice, Mum." Amy had opened the door without me noticing. "Let me do something with your hair. I could French pleat it for you, and your fringe could do with a trim."

I turned. "I'm off to karaoke night at the inn with Chrissy not some glamorous event."

Amy grinned at me. "Well, you never know who might be there. Live a little, Mum. Have fun. Sing terrible songs. Claire says Chrissy is great. We were chatting last night." Ralph wandered in and sat next to her. She patted his head.

"And don't worry, I'll sort the chickens out. Ralph loves herding them up even though they peck at him. Now, let's do your hair."

The bell rang bang on seven o'clock. I hurried to the door, grabbing my bag and coat. Chrissy had already returned to her car. I jumped into the passenger seat and shivered.

"It's colder than I thought," I said, wishing I'd chosen thicker tights.

"I'll turn on the heat." Warmth blossomed under my bottom and thighs. I wriggled into the seat.

"Oh, that's lovely. I wish my Range Rover had such heat. It's old but still useful in bad weather, being a four-by-four. I should get a newer one, but money is always tight."

"Your hair is nice."

"Amy insisted. She practically pushed me out of the door—says I don't have enough fun." *Why the hell did I say that?*

"Amy clearly talks sense." Chrissy set off. "Oh, by the way, I've found a few houses to view within twenty miles that are within my budget. Luckily, prices are lower up here than coastal Kent, so I've got a deposit. My problem will be proving a regular income, but I can rent for a while until I've proof enough."

"I can have a word with my ex if you want. He's an accountant. He does the farm's books—he's talented with numbers. If you need someone to do your books and show your previous income, he's your man." Yes, I had a cheek, but I knew he'd do it.

"I might take you up on that."

"Shit!" I grasped the seat.

"Sorry, I swerved to avoid a fox. Am I supposed to? Are there rules in the country?"

"At least it wasn't a deer or pheasants. A friend hit three of the buggers and wrote off her car. They wrecked the engine. Such stupid birds. They'll drop in front of you without warning, from over a hedge. We're nearly there. Pull in around the back."

The car park was almost full. Chrissy drove into a tight space, and we squeezed our way out then entered via the back door, along a few corridors to the bar.

"Bloody hell—it's busy," Chrissy said.

"Beth."

I turned to see Jed and Lars in the corner. Jed beckoned us over. "I grabbed Chrissy's arm. "You go over there, and I'll get us a drink. What do you want?"

"Just fizzy water. I don't drink and drive."

At the bar, Karen was busy. "Chrissy got you to come then, I see."

"She did. Usual please, and a fizzy water for Chrissy. The place is busy tonight."

"Karaoke still brings people in, especially when there's a fifty-pound voucher to spend anywhere in the village at stake. Will you be giving us your *I Will Survive*?"

"Not tonight. Maybe something else. Depends how many of these I drink." I picked up the glass of red, the water, and a menu then made my way over to the corner seat, took off my coat, and shuffled along the bench to sit next to Chrissy.

"I'm rubbish at history," Chrissy said. "Except for clothes. I could examine any costume and date it. I blame two things—firstly the *Ladybird book of Costume*, and secondly a grandmother who made costumes for the local amateur dramatics group. I learnt to sew and knit as soon as I could hold a needle. And your dress is wonderful, Beth—very fifties."

I grinned. I enjoyed the compliments.

"Funny you should mention that," Lars said. "We have an am-dram group, and we're always advertising for volunteers to help with costumes and props. You'd be more than welcome."

"Beware of these two," I said, handing over the menu. "They seem nice at first, then you'll find you've volunteered for something."

"Harsh," Jed muttered. "Just because you ended up doing a parachute jump for the local animal rescue."

"*You* did a *parachute* jump?" Chrissy said. "That is seriously impressive. I have trouble up ladders. I did a sponsored swim once, which reminds me. Is there a local pool?"

"There's the cold-water swimming group," Lars said. "I've been known to join them."

Chrissy shivered next to me. "Nah, I prefer to be warm. It's probably your Viking blood. Have you ordered?"

"Not yet. We'd better before it's karaoke time."

I checked the menu—it was pie night—and made orders for all of us. I wasn't sure what to sing. There was no chance of refusing, and I loved singing anyway. "I think I'll do *Wind Beneath my Wings*," I said.

"A song guaranteed to make me cry," Chrissy said. "I love the film."

"What are you going to give us?" Lars asked Chrissy. "Please don't say you have no voice."

"Mmm. I thought I might do *Running up that Hill*, as it's been back in the charts. I'm not sure I'm up to *Wuthering Heights*. What about you two?"

"We thought we might do *Under Pressure*—we've been practising."

I swallowed a large gulp of wine. "That's brave Jed, taking on those two fabulous voices."

"We're going all out for the win," Lars said. "Karen and George are performing *Islands in the Stream*. Though, of course they can't win the prize."

"Who's the judge?" Chrissy asked.

"Everyone decides. Whichever act gets the most votes wins the prize," I explained.

The food arrived and we dug into a variety of pies with veg and gravy. George, as always, made great pastry—flaky and light. I noticed at some point, Chrissy's thigh resting against mine.

73

She was tactile too, not afraid to let her fingers graze a leg or arm as she talked. I found myself wishing she'd touch me more, hanging on her every word. She had a great laugh and a sexy chuckle. I laughed at myself. *Who the hell has a sexy chuckle?* During the meal, Lars regaled us with stories of a recent school visit to the museum.

"Honestly, when one of the models moved, this teenager screamed his head off and ran, and another threw up because of the smells. They wouldn't have made Viking warriors, that's for certain."

"Not like you, my love." Jed leaned in and kissed Lars' bearded cheek. He smiled and stared at us. "Of course, he's forgotten how he threw up for the first few days of the cruise around the fjords we went on two years ago—he's no Viking sea-legs."

Lars flushed red under his auburn beard.

A glass tinkled at the bar and all heads turned. "Right, everyone. It's time for the main event of this evening—this month's karaoke challenge. While George and I give you our song for the evening, please fill your names in on the slips provided and put them in the hat. Singers will be drawn at random. The prize is the usual fifty-pound voucher—useful for buying those Easter eggs at this time of year. There is a great choice at the Post Office shop, I'm told."

A cheer sounded from the corner.

"It's run by locals," I whispered in Chrissy's ear, catching a whiff of expensive perfume.

Each of us filled in our slips.

First out of the hat from our table were Jed and Lars. They got the words muddled at one point, but gave a spirited rendition of a tricky song and received loud applause.

"And next out of the hat is Beth Nethering. Come on up, Beth."

I usually sang without care and without hope of winning, but knowing Chrissy liked this song from *Beaches* sent butterflies beating their wings in my stomach. I sat on the high stool and took a few deep breaths, listening to the introduction before I began. Emotion got the better of me at one point. My dad had always loved this song too and sang it to my mother. She was the one who'd always held things together. He'd said the farm couldn't function without her. I glanced across the room and saw Chrissy wipe away a tear. I'd had three glasses of wine by now, so maybe the alcohol was to blame for the emotional excess. I was glad when it was over. People clapped and I hurried back to my corner. Chrissy squeezed my thigh. Her touch was warm—it both settled and disturbed me.

After a couple of others had sung, she shifted next to me. "It must be my turn now."

"And last, but hopefully not least, we have new blood tonight. Joining us for the first time is Chrissy Wychling. Chrissy has opened the This is Me bridal shop at Nethering Farm. So anyone planning on getting hitched, you might want to visit. D'you want to come on up then, Chrissy."

She tensed beside me. "Go on," I whispered. "They'll be kind to you. I promise."

I waited as Chrissy had a word with Karen. When the music started I noticed her song choice had changed. When she sang *The Man with the Child in his Eyes*, her voice was pure and clear as a tinkling brook it was beautiful. I stared until Jed nudged me.

"Fucking hell. She's good," he whispered.

And she was. I and the rest of the room listened spellbound.

I had no doubt who would win. The cheers and whistles at the end left me in no doubt. I moved to let her sit in next to me.

"That was extraordinary," I said. "You could sing for a living."

Chrissy swallowed several large gulps of water. "Thank you. It's been years since I performed in front of strangers. I had singing lessons as a child and was in the local choir. I haven't sung properly in years. My ex was tone deaf—not her fault—but she wasn't a music lover. I didn't want her to think I was rubbing it in so stopped singing around her."

George rang the bell at the bar. "Right everyone, panic not, we've time until last orders, after that stunning performance, it's time to vote."

I stood and swayed. Chrissy caught me and I plonked back down. "I think I may have had more than I'm used to." Lars took the voting slips from me. George counted then made the announcement.

"And the winner is Chrissy Wychling."

"Wow. I wasn't expecting to win as I'm new here," Chrissy said. She collected the voucher from George and turned to address the crowd. "Thank you for your generosity. I'm sorry the outsider won, but maybe I'll get to be a local eventually."

Everyone applauded. ."

Later, getting back to the car, I still swayed even though the cool of the evening hit me. Chrissy smelled so good as she, Lars and Jed helped me into the front seat.

"I'll make sure she gets in all right," Chrissy assured them.

I sang all the way home. The world felt like a good place. I hoped I'd made a new friend. After I managed to get the key in the door, Chrissy assisted me to the kitchen.

"I'll make you a coffee," she said.

"No, my job." I insisted.

I stood none too steadily and she caught me in her arms. Our faces were inches away from each other. For the third time in my life, I let my heart rule my head—I kissed her. Her lips were warm. I couldn't remember the last time I'd kissed anyone. She held me. I pressed harder, letting my lips open, and she followed me. After all the evening's little touches, I wanted more.

At the sound of footsteps on the stairs, I sprang away. The kitchen door opened. I wiped my mouth as if the kiss might have left an obvious trace and turned to the kettle. I'd almost forgotten that Amy would be there.

"You're home, then," Amy said. "Good night, was it?"

"Yes," I said, attempting to collect my thoughts while Chrissy stood, saying nothing. "Chrissy won the karaoke prize."

She touched my arm. "And I'd better get going. No time for coffee—busy day tomorrow. I'll see myself out. Thanks for this evening."

I watched her go. What had I done?

# 10. Chrissy

Two days went by—two busy days—and I hadn't seen Beth nor heard from her. I'd gone over that moment so many times wondering what might have happened if Amy hadn't come in when she did. I told myself I'd have been the better person knowing Beth was towards the drunker end of tipsy as well as lonely. In a way, Amy had done us both a favour. While sipping coffee, I glanced at the designs I'd sketched for Izzy. The dress itself was waiting for her to try on. I'd been up until the early hours making the final alterations. We had fifteen minutes before she arrived.

Every so often, rain pattered on the window, preparing us for the onset of April showers. Claire was positioned at the entrance with a large umbrella. I drank the last of my coffee and told myself Beth would speak to me when she was good and ready. I had other things on my mind, and I needed to focus.

"She's here," Claire said, poking her head through after opening the door. I followed her into the showroom then stood and waited. Making a one-off dress like this could be expensive if the bride didn't like what I'd done. The doors opened and

Izzy wheeled herself in followed by her brother, James, and another person who I guessed might be Mum. Her black Labrador walked at the side of her chair. We exchanged hellos and introductions until Izzy was ready to follow me into the changing area. The others, plus dog, waited in the main room while Claire made tea then came to help me.

"Okay" I said. "Before the reveal, I want to explain the idea. The skirt and lace cover are detachable from each other. The skirt also has a fold over front with a clip at the side. You'll be able to open it up and transfer over and back and do it up again without having to take off the whole dress. The bodice is simple. We'll check the fit today. I've allowed room for your arms to move so nothing is torn when you wheel yourself. The arms are also detachable and covered with the same lace as the skirt. The dress is strapless, but I have extra choices if you want to add them." I hoped I'd considered everything. The dress had to be functional but also this was a wedding dress—it needed to be special too.

"Ready for the reveal?"

Izzy nodded.

Claire entered as I pulled the cover from the mannequin.

For a moment. Izzy simply stared. Claire glanced at me. I held onto the desk and crossed my fingers.

"The colour on the lace is perfect," Izzy said. "I love how you've used small purple flowers like I asked. I wanted colour. Can I try it on?"

"Of course. It's why you're here." Through a process of transferring from chair to chair and all of us working together, the dress was fitted. Izzy decided to leave her shoulders bare.

"In my bag," she said. "I've an amethyst necklace that was my great-grandmother's." It fit perfectly.

"Now for the big test. I'm pushing myself down the aisle with my dad beside me."

I nodded at Claire who hurried through to tell the others to close their eyes.

Izzy pushed herself through the doors without mishap. "Close your eyes. Is it okay if I push you into place?"

"It's fine. Shit, I'm nervous."

I altered her position, so she was in front of the mirror. Once again, I crossed my fingers.

"You can open your eyes." Everyone gasped, the dog sat up, and I waited.

"Mum?" Izzy said.

Tears poured over her mother's face. It's incredible. The dress is beautiful, darling, like you, but is it practical?"

Izzy nodded. "Chrissy has sorted everything. I'll even be able to use the loo without a huge performance."

"Are you happy with it?" I asked. "We still have time to alter anything."

"No. I don't want to change a thing, though I might want a short veil."

I reached behind and Claire passed me the veil made of the same lace with a matching purple headband. I placed it on Izzy's head and the outfit was complete. Claire handed round the tissues.

"That dress is spectacular, sis. Maybe we could get a veil in the same lace for Bella too."

Everyone smiled. Bella, the labrador, looked unimpressed.

"When you're ready, I'll get everything boxed up for you."

"And you'll be able to come on the day to help?" Izzy asked.

"It would be a privilege. All part of the package."

An hour later, we waved goodbye, and I accompanied Claire

back to the office. "Are you sure you'll be all right on your own?" I asked.

"I'll be fine if anyone arrives on spec. I know the stock, and I can make appointments for them to return. You go and check out those houses. Places get snapped up quickly around here. It's been a good day so far, so ride the tide. One of those you're seeing today might be perfect."

"All right but call me and I'll return. I'm off to get changed first. I'll be back before five."

Back at the pod, I changed out of my suit into jeans and jumper with sensible boots. If any of these places was suitable, I'd be glad to have my own stuff around me once more, and all the extra space—though I'd miss the hot tub. I turned at a knock on the door.

"Come in," I called out.

It opened and Beth stood in the doorway. I stayed sitting on the bed waiting for her to say something. She opened her mouth, but the words clearly froze, and she coughed.

"I'm sorry."

"What about?" Clearly, I could guess, but, well, she hadn't called me for the last two days, and she'd initiated the kiss, not me. I didn't intend to accept the part of the wicked temptress.

She rolled back on her heels then reached out to support herself. "About Wednesday night."

"When you kissed me."

"Yes, when I kissed you."

I waited, knowing what was coming.

"I'd had too much to drink." And there it was—the excuse of excuses. I hesitated on how to answer.

"Look, I don't want to let this get in the way of us being friends. It was a moment—that's all. Claire said you were off house-hunting this afternoon. I hope it's not because... I mean you are welcome to stay as long as you need." She paused. "I wondered if you'd like company. I know lots of people and places around here. I could help, you know, and make sure you're not ripped off. If you wanted."

I had to admit, having a local with me could be useful. "It's rented property I'm viewing—you know, a six-month lease, then hope I can prove enough income to buy, if things go okay."

"Claire says everything is going well so far. And you've left her on her own this afternoon. I think she appreciates your trust in her."

"She's a fast learner and keen. She has my number." I swallowed hard. "And having someone with me this afternoon would be useful." I didn't want to lose Beth's friendship either, or she was still my landlady. "I've three places to see. Let's forget Wednesday for now. We all do stupid things in the heat of the moment, but it doesn't mean I didn't want to be kissed, or in that moment, that you wanted to kiss me. You might want to think about that sometime." I wasn't letting her off the hook so easily.

"I'm not arguing," she said.

"We'd better get off then. The first place is in Bedale."

We didn't talk much. Spring was beginning to show itself. Daffodils lined many of the roads and lambs frolicked in the fields. On the hedges, there were the first signs of leaves. Buds had even started forming on the trees. Soon everything would be green again.

"It should be the next right," Beth said. I'd given her the job of navigating the way.

"I bet it's that one." A tell-tale flashy car sat outside the property. The *To Rent* sign also helped work out which one. I parked the car, and we climbed out at the same time as someone wearing a three-piece suit exited the other car. I stepped forward first.

He held out his hand. "Ms Wychling. It's good to meet you. My name is Carl Mattingley."

"It's Chrissy," I said. "And this is Beth who is helping me find the perfect place."

A grin crossed his features. "Hi, Beth. It's been a few years."

"I said I knew people," she said. "I was in school with Carl's sister. You going to give us the details then?"

I knew as soon as I walked in the door this place wasn't for me. It was sterile, which I suppose was good in some ways. It was clean, but new—too new. I followed him around anyway letting him talk.

"There's a parking space at the back, but no garden."

I hadn't realised I wanted one until the moment I'd stared at the tarmacked area at the back. Carl was astute enough to notice.

"I'm guessing this one isn't for you. I think you might like the next property better. I'll meet you there."

"He was right. It wasn't me," I said to Beth in the car. "It was featureless—like all those rented properties you see on TV programmes—all grey and white, and all the same. It's an old cottage made into something it isn't. It felt sad. Let's get to the next one. It's the other side of Netherington and it appeared nicely decorated online. It also had tiny walled garden."

We parked a few metres away from the house on the village green. I suspected when everyone was home, parking might be at a premium, but that didn't bother me. This place was old. Carl met us again. We stepped into a hallway with stairs leading up and a corridor leading to the kitchen at the back. The main room was decorated with warmer colours—creams and peaches. The fire was modern but surrounded by older tiles and a wooden mantlepiece. The window had a deep wooden sill, suggesting the walls were as wide. It was cosy but would be big enough for my furniture.

"There's a loo under the stairs," Carl explained. "The kitchen was fitted a few years back, and you'll have all the useful features like washing machine, fridge, oven and hob, and even a dishwasher. Outside, there's a small, enclosed garden with a few pots, giving you somewhere to sit. I'm told the honeysuckle is rampant in summer."

Upstairs, were two bedrooms and a bathroom. The biggest, at the back, had views over the hills.

"I'll take it," I said.

"Are you sure?" Beth asked. "You have the other one to see."

"I can cancel the appointment," Carl said. "We can sort everything out and have you in here as soon as you like. I'll let the owner know."

"I've decided," I said. "This place has a good feeling."

We waved goodbye to Carl. "Are you sure?" Beth asked.

"I'm one of these people who knows straight away, although I have been known to make mistakes, this is only for six months. That'll hopefully give me enough time to sort out proof for a mortgage lender. And Carl did say the lease could be extended. I'll also be able to pick Claire up on the way to work and drop her off, making life easier." I glanced at the house once more. "It'll be perfect. Talking about Claire, we'd better get back there. Thank you for coming with me."

"In fairness, I didn't do much."

"But he knew you, which helped."

"I suppose so."

Back at the farm, Beth followed me into the bridal barn. We found Claire sitting in the office. She had a huge grin on her face.

"I sold a dress," she said. "Someone came in to see what we had and found a dress she liked. She tried it on, and it was perfect for her, and needed no alterations. She paid and took it with her. I'm entering the details now."

I hugged her shoulders. "That's fantastic, Claire. Believe me, it doesn't happen every day. And I've found somewhere to rent the other side of Netherington. I'll be able to give you a lift, which will save your mum time."

"A good day for us both." A car horn beeped from outside. "That'll be Mum now. I'll see you Monday." She grabbed her coat and practically skipped off.

Beth stared at me. "I was wondering," she said. "If you're not opening tomorrow, maybe you could join me for a picnic in the afternoon. We're supposed to have a mini heatwave for the next couple of days and I'd like to show you the farm if you're interested."

Was I letting myself in for a load of trouble? Maybe. The memory of our first kiss lingered. I hoped for more but would let Beth move at her own pace. I had no idea what was going on in her head. "I'd love to," I said.

"I'll use the quad bike so jeans and boots would be best and a coat as it can get quite breezy on the tops."

"I'll dress appropriately," I said.

She moved from foot to foot. "I'll pick you up tomorrow around two then. That'll give us a few hours and we can find somewhere sheltered to have high tea. I'll get off now. I've baking to do. I hope you like scones."

"I love scones, savoury or sweet."

"Good. Then two o' clock it is."

She turned and headed for the door, giving me one shy glance before escaping to the outside. I had a date—well, a sort of date. I wasn't rushing anything. I needed Beth to come to me if she was going to. Turning her life upside down, which she might well be doing, was a huge decision only she could make.

# 11. Beth

I spent the morning doing all my usual chores. The house got a tidy with Amy being away for Easter at her father's house. It was always strange without her, and Ralph moped about the place without his favourite human. I also baked two batches of scones and a loaf of bread then played hunt the cool bag. Once found, I packed it with the scones, ham sandwiches, home-made pickle, sheep's cheese—our own—jam and cream, along with fizzy water and a flask of tea. After the last time, I decided against alcohol. Jed walked in as I inserted the cool packs into the bag.

"Going somewhere?" he asked, nodding at the bag.

"As a matter of fact, I'm taking Chrissy on a tour of the farm, and we're having a picnic." *I sound defensive.*

He sat at the table.

"Have you nothing to do?" I asked.

"Nope. The sheep are sorted. Dad and I moved them to one of the out fields where we prepared the grass last year. The lambs are fed and running around. We should be able to get them outside soon. The milk levels were good. The tanker will be here to collect tomorrow. Simon told me yesterday another string of small supermarkets has shown interest in the yoghurt and cheese. Also, the costs for the ice cream production system are in so there's a meeting next week. He said he sent you an email."

"Yes, I got it and put it in my diary. By the way, I'm thinking of getting a couple more glamping pods if I can sort the services out. We're making money on them now. We had a booking come in yesterday for a weekend at the beginning of May so one of the party can try on dresses at Chrissy's bridal barn. They're coming from Newtonmore in the Highlands, would you believe?"

"Back to you and Chrissy," Jed said. "You do know she's gay, don't you?"

I bristled, took a breath, and zipped up the bag for something to do with my hands. "And what's that got to do with the price of fish?" I asked.

"She's recently come out of a marriage."

"I know."

"You don't want to give her the wrong idea."

My temper flared. I couldn't help myself. "Excuse me. But how am I giving her the wrong idea, oh wise one? We've been to karaoke night at the pub, and I'm showing her the farm. She's on her own here. I'm simply trying to be a friend."

"Exactly. She's lonely and you're lonely. Don't deny it. And there was the one time in university you told me about— snogging some girl to make Graham jealous. I seem to remember you kind of liked it."

I stood with arms folded, knowing how it looked. "It was once, and it served its purpose. Next you'll be telling me gay people can't be friends with people of the same sex, which coming from you is a bit much. I can assure you that there are hundreds of men out in the big wide word who I wouldn't touch with a barge pole."

Jed grinned. "Me too." He picked up a spare scone and bit into it. "These are good even without butter. Chrissy is in for a treat." He took another bite.

I glanced at my watch.

"I like Chrissy, you know. She seems like fun, and you two were pretty touchy-feely at the pub." Jed, as usual, had a point. He didn't miss much. He was one of my oldest friends. I didn't like lying to him, and I knew I could trust him. I sat at the table.

"You know I haven't had anything to do with women in that way—just a few fleeting thoughts. I mean every girl has a crush on someone when they're young, don't they? I know you fancied your teachers. You used to go on about Mr Evans and his gorgeous arse."

Jed sighed. "It was magnificent. He was sweet too. I found out years later that he is gay. He was on that cruise to the fjords with his husband, you know, the one I went on with Lars a few years back. He still had the arse."

I took a deep breath. I needed to come clean to someone and Jed was the obvious choice. "I kissed her."

Jed slammed his fist on the table. "I knew it. You kept staring at her. And?"

"And Amy came in. She didn't see anything. Chrissy and I talked about it yesterday. I don't know what to do, Jed. I'm nearly forty. I run a complicated business in a rural area. I have a teenage daughter—"

"Who'll be leaving home to go to university soon. What do you want to do?"

"*I* don't know. Really, I have *no* idea. The kiss was good, but it's been so long since I kissed anyone, let alone another woman. She asked me not to mess her around. But what if I did?"

"Only you and her can decide on that. You could always try friends with benefits."

I sighed. "Maybe I need the friend not the benefits."

"Karen's your friend, and you've never fancied her, have you?"

I laughed out loud. "Ye Gods. Karen would eat me alive." He grinned. "Stop it," I said.

"Did you miss sex when you and Graham divorced?"

"Truth?" I asked. "I didn't miss sex while we were together. I did begin to wonder if I was asexual. But when I kissed Chrissy —I knew. If she'd have responded... If Amy hadn't come in... I don't know."

"So go out this afternoon and see how things are with her. You only get this life, Chrissy. They say life begins at forty. Take a chance. You never know. And now, after my words of wisdom, I will leave you. I'm making dinner tonight. Lars will be hungry after a day at the museum playing a Viking. If I'm lucky, he'll want his wicked way with me. I told him to keep the costume on."

I grinned. Jed could always make me laugh. I picked up the bag, put food out for Ralph, and locked up behind me. The sun was warm on my face and the breeze was gentle. I could smell spring in the air. I picked up an extra helmet for Chrissy and sat astride the quad bike. She'd have to hold on tight.

I found Chrissy sitting on the bench on the veranda of the pod reading. I envied her. I couldn't remember the last time I'd picked up a book. I needed to do something about that. She glanced up as I approached.

"What are you reading?" I asked.

"It's a crime novel set in Victorian England with two women detectives—like a female version of Holmes and Watson. The writer gives incredible descriptions of the muck and grime when compared to polite society. They somehow lived side-by-side. Is the helmet for me?"

"It is. We're using the quad bike. You can sit behind me, but you'll need to hold on."

She stood, placed the book back in the pod, took the helmet, and followed me back to our transport. "I suppose you've been driving one of these for years," she said with a doubtful expression.

"I have. Here, let me make sure the helmet is secure." I stepped in close enough to smell her shampoo—citrus and something else I wasn't sure of. I checked the strap under her chin and stepped back.

"Very fetching." I secured mine and climbed on the bike. She sat behind me. "I won't go fast," I shouted. "You have to be careful with these things, especially when there's a trailer attached. The hay is for the Highland coos. I thought you might like to see them first." I switched on the engine and headed through the farm to the open fields. Ned waved us through the gate among the sheep he was guiding back out from the milking parlour. I drove to the top of the field and stopped to watch Ned at work with his dogs.

"Take your headgear off," I said. "It's easier to talk." I could feel the heat from her body behind me and her breath on my neck.

"Those dogs are amazing," Chrissy said. "And the way Ned directs them using a few whistles and hand signals."

"They're mother and son," I said. "Champions both. They could probably do this on their own. This is what we call the intake field nearest the farm. Because we milk them, we have to bring them in every day. Like cows, they seem to know when to gather, which makes life easier. They know Ned and Jed as well."

"Don't they say sheep can recognise up to fifteen faces?"

"They do. They can be stubborn beasts as well. Luckily, they also have a habit of following each other, which also helps. Ned is taking them to a higher field. We're trying something new with the grass to save on hay this year. I won't bore you with the details. Jed is keen on innovations. His father usually talks about the old days then becomes incredibly proud of his boy."

"How did Jed's parents react to him being gay?"

"His mother cried for ten seconds, and his father shrugged. Ned isn't one for words. They love Lars anyway. Jed says if he and Lars ever split up they'd probably want to keep Lars. Shall we move on? The cows are in the field by the lane where you turn into your barn."

I drove though the fields, opening and closing gates then along the side of the footpath. Hedges lined the roads. No doubt birds would already be nesting. We didn't get too close to the small herd. I jumped off and threw out the hay, knowing they'd amble over.

"The babies are so gorgeous and fluffy," Chrissy said.

"They are. We had this big old bull when I was little. Dad used to put me on his back and lead him around. Sadly, Jethro is long gone now. These days we use artificial insemination. All four of our girls got pregnant this year. The other two should give birth any day now. They stay outside all year round, even in snow."

"I didn't realise they came in colours other than ginger."

"Anywhere from cream to black," I explained.

We sat and watched them lumber around then followed the path again to the higher fields, where the stone walls seemed to stretch forever. I intended to take Chrissy to the highest point on our land—funny I still thought of it as ours not mine—where you could see most of the farm and across to the other side of the dale. Through the middle ran a river which formed the boundary between us and the neighbours. At this stage on its journey, it still had some speed. Lethargy set in lower down the valley where the river meandered to the sea. Twenty minutes later, after driving across several fields and opening and closing gates, we reached the top where a patch of trees had hung on in an area that was once all forest. As a child, my brother Neil and I had climbed these trees and strung a Tarzan rope from one of the thicker branches. We'd sat among the leaves and Neil had told me all his plans for the farm when it became his—so many plans. I hoped he'd be happy with what I'd done with the place. With Ned and Jed's help, I'd set up a stone table, so I'd have somewhere to sit, eat, and think. Sometimes, I sat on the table and contemplated the universe I found myself in —one I'd certainly not entertained when I was sitting as a child in those trees. Back then, all I wanted was bright lights and big city.

"We're stopping here," I said. Chrissy let go of my waist. I got off and grabbed two folding chairs from the trailer. "I've brought a picnic. We can sit here." I picked up the bag and set out the chairs while Chrissy climbed off the bike and stood and stared.

"It's so neat," she said. "With all those defined fields with their stone walls and trees dotted around the place. Some of the walls appear as if they're hanging on to the sides."

"Building them is a skilled job," I said. "And like so many countryside jobs there are less people with the skills to do them."

Chrissy strolled over and sat in the chair next to me so we both could admire the view. "I love how you can see the rivulets where the water runs off the hills and begins its journey to the sea—everything connected. This is a lovely place," she said. "It feels special."

"It is. My brother and I used to come here as kids and sit in the trees."

"You've not said much about him. I don't even know his name."

"No, his name was Neil. I used to tease him even though he was older than me and call him Nellie. His ashes are buried under the horse chestnut tree. He carved his initials on that one. My father and grandfather and others are also on there. These trees are old." I think they were planted by one of my ancestors. I'm not sure what they'd make of having a woman in charge of the place."

"Your mother's still alive though, isn't she? Claire mentioned her briefly."

I opened the bag without answering and placed various food containers on the stone table. Luckily, even up here the breeze was slight today. I glanced at the sky. A bird hovered above the hilltop.

"Watch," I said, pointing over the valley. "It's a hen harrier. Any minute now it'll plummet to catch something." We gazed at it until it swooped into the grass and came away with something in its talons.

"It probably has a nest somewhere near," I explained. I was conscious I'd avoided Chrissy's question. I hadn't intended to.

"My mother lives in France. She moved there twelve years ago when my father became ill. He was told to retire, and to make sure he did, she found a place in the Loire valley. It's when Neil took over the farm. Dad had a heart condition. Farming is a stressful job. We're always trying to balance the books with loans, subsidies, and grants. Dad had a quadruple by-pass, but the damage had been too great and heart disease got him in the end. I thought Mum would come back here, but she stayed in France with her new friends—she calls them the Widow's Club. I didn't blame her—still don't. She has a new man-friend. We go over to visit when we can."

"I expect holidays are difficult with a farm to run."

"They are, but I'm lucky to have Ned and Jed. Jed does most of the farm management on a day-to-day basis with a few part-time hands. He's the one with the agricultural management degree. I do all the contracts and legal stuff and find us sources of money where I can. I help out around the farm and with the animals, but it wasn't my plan to be a hands-on farmer."

"And yet you're here."

"I am." I gazed across over the fields which had been in my family for so long and took a deep breath. "In my life, I've let my heart rule my head on three occasions. The second of those was coming back here and ending my marriage when Neil died."

Chrissy placed her hand on my arm. I stared at it, feeling the warmth of the connection while I desperately attempted to swallow the lump in my throat. Even after ten years, the words were difficult to get out.

"You don't have to tell me," Chrissy said. "We can simply sit here, eat this food, and stare at the view."

I picked up the flask and poured two mugs of tea—typically British. "No, I want to tell you before someone else does. When Neil took over the farm, things didn't go well. Graham, my husband showed me the books. We were haemorrhaging money. I tried to talk to Neil, but he wouldn't listen. He wanted to farm in the same way Dad had done, but there's no money in sheep farming It cost more to shear the sheep than the fleeces brought in. The bank refused to give him another loan." I paused and sipped the tea. "Then the accident happened. It had rained for days. His car slid off a narrow track into an overflowing beck." Her grip on my arm tightened. "It took the search party hours to find the car. He drowned. The inquest gave accident as the cause of death, but people gossiped when we found out he'd taken out a big life insurance policy a two years before. The truth is, I'll never know. He'd left the farm to me. Mum wanted nothing to do with it. Around the same time, I found out Graham had been cheating on me, though I've never told him I knew, so I decided to come back, and brought Amy with me."

"You've made a success of the place, though." Chrissy said.

"Yes, I introduced lots of changes working with others, spreading the financial load, and diversifying. It's not always been easy. Our first breakthrough was getting the supermarket contract for the yoghurt and cheese. Contracts are my speciality. I do all the legal work for our company—saves us a fortune."

Chrissy placed her hand over mine. "I'm sorry about your brother. Rob is my twin and we're close. Coming here was hard for me after my marriage broke up, especially leaving Rob. But he's married to a great woman who will be the making of him."

She paused. "Any chance of something to eat? I didn't have lunch."

"Sorry. Of course. There are ham sandwiches, samples of our cheeses, savoury and sweet scones, home-made chutney, jam, and cream." I opened the containers, and we tucked in. Chrissy moaned when she bit into a sandwich.

"This bread is amazing, and the ham is real, and butter. I can't remember the last time I ate real butter. Is it all local?"

"Every bit. I made the bread. The ham comes from a local farm, as does the butter. I made the scones, the chutney, and the jam." I still amazed myself when I thought about how I'd have bought all those things in the past. "We make several types of cheese, from soft enough to spread, to a hard cheese which has a nutty flavour. There's also a blue version. Our cheese production manager, Angelina, is a genius—Italian. Her brother is helping us create the new ice cream collection. People are eating more sheep milk because of its anti-inflammatory properties."

Chrissy spread soft cheese on a savoury scone. "This is so nice. And this is too, sitting here with you on a sunny day, smelling the fresh air." She finished the scone, wiped her mouth, and turned to face me.

"You said there were three times you'd let your heart rule your head. Can I ask what the others were?"

I poured another mug of proper Yorkshire tea and swallowed a few mouthfuls. *In for a penny...* "The first was deciding to keep my baby. When I got pregnant, Graham and I were engaged. He'd been working for a large accountancy firm and had recently been promoted. I had a place in a fabulous and progressive chambers in central London. We'd found a property we could afford, and the wedding was three months away. It was not the right time for a baby, but I wanted her. She'd fought her way into existence through a condom and the Pill. My boss was great—totally supportive of my choice. She brought me back part-time. We coped. That was the first time."

"And the third occasion?" Chrissy met my gaze. I swallowed.

"The third occasion was when I kissed you."

# 12. Chrissy

I had no idea how to reply to this declaration, so I didn't. In the last hour or so, I'd found out how Beth's father and brother had died, how she'd made the choice to leave her marriage and successful career to return home to a farm in trouble, and how she'd turned the situation around. The woman was a hero. All I'd done was deal with a cheating partner and moved as far away as possible from those circumstances.

"You haven't said anything," Beth said, interrupting my thoughts.

"No. I'm sorry. Truthfully, I was thinking how courageous you've been doing…" I waved my arms around. "Well, taking on all this and making a success of it."

"You've taken a chance too. Opening a bridal shop for a special type of client in the middle of nowhere might be considered foolish by some people."

"My family think I've gone mad," I said. "But I had to try." Yes, I was ignoring the elephant in the room. I wasn't sure what to think. I mean, I had flirted with Beth. Why wouldn't I? I knew my type and she was it. Finding out more about the sort of woman she was only increased my desire to know her better.

"Sometimes, you have to take a leap into the unknown." Beth's words brought me back out of my head. I gazed at her wondering what she'd say next.

"For me, coming back here was coming home. Having a baby and kissing you were infinitely scarier."

"I'm not sure how to answer you, if that was even a question."

"Both were something new. I'd had little to do with babies —well, human ones—and this tiny crying creature arrived expecting me to know what to do and how to take care of her."

"You seem to have done a good job."

Beth smiled, creating dimples. I wanted to hug her so much. Tears formed in the corner of each eye. She wiped them on her sleeve. "Thank you. I'm so proud of her. We have our disagreements—she's a teenager so that's usual—but she loves this place. She's much more attached to the land than I ever was. As a child, I once caught her plunging her hands into a muddy puddle. She took her time to grow taller so was hoping if she stuck her hands in the ground it would help her grow like the plants and animals here."

I chuckled. "Well, at least she didn't try eating the grass. I think we always want to be different to who we are. It's the human condition—never to be satisfied, or I suppose we'd have remained in the Rift Valley in Africa still afraid of climbing over the hill to find out what was there."

"It would be bloody crowded by now."

"It would," I agreed.

"I haven't kissed a woman before," she said, staring out over the fields. "I'd thought about it once or twice, but I've never been one for jumping into bed with someone I've just met or one-night stands. I need to feel a connection." She paused.

I waited for her to continue.

"Me and Graham were friends first—part of a group. In hindsight, I should have left it at that, but I liked him, and we got along. The sex was good, or so I thought having nothing to compare to—you know, straightforward. I didn't feel I was missing anything. Amy coming along when she did changed everything in my life." She reached into her pocket, took out her phone, and stared at the photo of her daughter.

"I loved her so much, and Graham and I drifted apart. If the farm hadn't come back into my life, I don't think we'd have survived as a couple anyway. We're far better as friends. Over the last few years, Karen has set me up on a few dates until she gave in as well." She turned to face me.

"Then you came along. That night in the hot tub made me think. I had all sorts of questions demanding answers. It was nice, exciting, to be flirted with. Later, lying in bed, I thought about you—I created my own little fantasy. With the kiss, after a few drinks, I was tipsy enough to test fantasy with reality."

I shifted in the chair, my stomach squirmed, and my pulse quickened. I was afraid to ask how fantasy and reality compared.

"If Amy hadn't come in when she did. I'm not sure what would have happened. She's away for Easter at her father's, by the way. I'm in the house alone, except for Ralph."

Was she saying what I thought she was saying? "Do you want to try more kissing?" I asked. The words escaped my mouth before my brain had chance to stop them.

"I think so. I don't know about anything else though. Would you like to have dinner with me. I've made a casserole.

We could sit on the sofa, watch a film, and see what happens. Would that be all right?"

*She's not out. This could all fall apart. You'll have to live here if it does.* I had a list of valid reasons why this was madness. "That sounds perfectly lovely," I said.

---

Before we got to the sofa, there were chores to do. Ralph needed a run around. I laughed as Beth set up a machine which threw balls for him to chase. Ralph had no trouble amusing himself while we gathered the chickens and ducks into their houses for the night.

"That's everything," Beth said, having checked on the motherless lambs. "I don't know about you, but I'm starving."

We sat on the sofa in the cosy living room with steaming hot bowls of beef casserole on trays on our laps. I took one mouthful and sighed. The beef fell apart in my mouth. "This is beautiful," I said.

"I use a slow cooker. Days can be busy, so I throw everything in then leave it."

"Do you ever have take-aways out here?" I thought of the Italian, Chinese, and Indian meals I'd eaten over the years. I wasn't a cook.

"There's a chippie in the village does great fish and chips. It's been known for us to eat take-out on a Friday. I do a big supermarket shop every few weeks and keep a lot in the chest freezer. Mum taught me to cook what she called proper English food, which is ironic considering how much she loves French cuisine now." She shifted and tucked her legs under her body.

"What about your family? What do they do?"

"My dad is a plumber. My mum is an assistant manager in a supermarket hoping to retire soon. My brother builds websites —he did mine. He got married recently."

"And your childhood? Was it fun living so near the sea with London so easy to get to?"

I stared across the room. "It was. I do miss the beaches. London was exciting, but I don't miss the noise and bustle. My wife loved it. My childhood was happy. My parents love each other and love us. I had friends. I didn't mind school. All boringly normal. I found what I loved early on. I think it helps —knowing what you're interested in and being able to follow your dreams. A lot of my friends had no idea and went to university for something to do. I adore my job. I like to think I make people happy, and not everyone can say that."

"No, they can't. Do you want any more to eat? Or I've a few of our yoghurts."

"I'm curious to see if they taste different—surprise me."

I watched Beth unfold her limbs, stretch, then stand and make her way out of the room. I glanced around. The walls were covered in photographs and paintings of people, animals, and landscapes There were two big sofas covered in knitted throws, a coffee table, a couple of large bookcases filled with actual books, though most of them looked old and many were bound in leather, and a display cabinet full of cups, rosettes, ornaments, and all sorts of what my mother would call clutter. A wood-burning fire, which I guessed had been around longer than fashion demanded, stood in one corner, with a TV in another. It felt like a room to relax in with your feet on the sofa after a long day, not a place in which to be careful about what you touched. Beth returned, followed by Ralph at her heels. He hopped onto the other sofa, closed his eyes, and went to sleep.

"Here, this is toffee flavour," Beth said, handing me a spoon. I dipped it in and tasted. "It's good—smooth and still creamy. I like Greek-style with it being thicker," I said. I placed the empty tub on the table once I'd finished.

"Right," I said. "If I remember rightly, there was mention of more kissing. How about we start now?" I moved closer to Beth, put my hands either side of her face, and leaned in.

Our lips met and the hairs rose on the back of my neck. Kissing her was like both coming home and being in the most exciting place on Earth, with a little scary thrown in for good measure. We both opened our lips a fraction. I turned my head and let my tongue seek more contact. Our mouths were open now. She moved her hands behind me to pull me even closer. Her tongue sought mine. I'd have been happy to do this all night, but , I eased away holding onto her bottom lip until I couldn't anymore.

Beth stared at me. "Wow. That was..."

Before I had chance to say anything, she kissed me again, wrapping her arms around me She ran her hands up and down my spine, pushed her tongue in to meet mine. I moved my hand to cup her breast and she moaned into my mouth. If we kept this up, my knickers would be wet through in minutes. Bloody hell, this woman could kiss. She stopped. Our faces were still only inches apart.

"I want more," she said. "I want more of this." She pressed my hand to her chest. "I want more of you. I want to see more of you. I want to hold you in my arms. I want to make you feel good. Please tell me you want the same."

I nodded. "Please," I said. "Take me to bed."

Beth stood and reached out her hand to me. I grabbed it and she led me out of the room and up the stairs to her room.

She switched on a bedside lamp, which sent a warm glow across the space and closed the curtains. I waited, following her lead. She glanced at me.

"I need the loo. Please sit. I won't be long."

I sat and checked out the space hoping Beth wouldn't change her mind between the bathroom and returning here. We hadn't crashed into the bedroom ripping each other's clothes off like they do in movies, giving me time to take in my surroundings. Beth's room was cheerful with lots of rainbow colours and old-fashioned wood furniture that had some age, though the bed felt new. I sank into the mattrass and waited. When the door opened, I held my breath. Beth strode across the floor to stand in front of me. I gazed at her, listening to us both breathing. Outside, an owl hooted. I leaned forward, lay my head on her chest, and wrapped my arms around her back. Beth ran her fingers through my hair.

"I've no idea what to do," Beth said. "Should we undress and get into bed and see what happens?"

Our eyes met when I glanced up. I undid my waistcoat and slipped it from my shoulders, then my shirt, leaving my bra. Beth pulled off her jumper, revealing pale skin with smatterings of freckles gained long ago. Her bra was functional and white.

"It opens at the front," she said. I took the cue and undid each hook, letting each cup fall. Her nipples were full and dark pink. Maybe it was the cool air that, hardened them or desire. I didn't care. I longed to take them between my lips and suck them or squeeze her breasts between my hands. Instead, I was near enough to reach a nub with the tip of my tongue.

Beth shook out her hair and moaned.

"Yes. Please. More."

I sucked hard, without warning.

"Oh, God, yes. That feeling is almost too exquisite to bare."

I buried my face between them. I sucked one nipple then sucked the other while I pushed my hands down the back of her jeans to hold her arse. I loved the soft curve of each cheek.

"Need to lie down," Beth said.

We removed the rest of our clothes at speed and slipped under the duvet wearing just our knickers. Beth moved into my arms, reached out and held one my nipples.

"They're lighter than mine," she said. "And this one has a crease in it."

"Yes," I murmured. "It always has. It's not as sensitive as the other one."

She settled her mouth near enough to flick out her tongue then took my nipple in her mouth and sucked hard while her palm lay on my stomach moving in circles and slowly getting wider and wider, dipping under my knickers. After a few minutes of her licking, sucking, and biting, and me writhing under her touch feeling the damp pour out of me, she stopped and stared at me.

"I want to touch you," she said. "But am I rushing? I don't want to rush."

"There aren't any rules," I said. "There also aren't any limits. If you want to touch me then touch me. I want to feel you explore."

"Can I see too? I want to see my hands touching you. I want to see you. Is that all right?"

I threw the duvet over, wriggled out of my knickers and opened my legs. Beth sat next to me and stared then she kissed me on the mouth, my neck, my breasts, and placed little soft, warm kisses all the way down my body until she reached below my belly button.

"You don't shave all your hair off," she said. "I don't either." She slipped her hand between my legs and lay her head on my tummy. I lay back feeling her touch, feeling each separate digit move while I ran my own fingers through her hair. I knew I was damp.

"I love watching my fingers disappear between the folds." She touched my clit and my body lurched. She pressed hard then moved in slow circles.

"Good?" she asked.

"It is," I said, feeling my body respond. My pelvis lifted to get more, but I didn't want this to be quick. She shifted her hand and placed her thumb on my clit and pushed a finger inside me then another. I reached down and held onto Beth's arse squeezing as my climax grew. She fucked me gently.

"So beautiful. You are so beautiful. I want to make you come."

"Don't stop," I managed between quickening breaths.

"I don't intend to. I want to feel you come around my fingers. Don't you pull away from me."

My body tightened. Inside, it felt as if something was trying to escape. The feeling gathered and gathered, every muscle tensed, and then I came.

"Oh hell." I gripped her arse, letting the contractions continue until I could stand no more. "Enough, please."

She stopped and eased out of me then lay her face lower and breathed in. "You smell amazing. Next time, I want to bury my face in all that wet."

I shuddered at her words, a little overwhelmed. She moved to sit up, then sat astride me, and leaned in to kiss me. I had no words yet. Somehow, this woman had discovered the core of me at her first attempt.

"Are you all right?" she asked with a worried expression.

I smiled. "I'm glorious."

She glowed in the half-light. Her nipples stood hard and dark and I reached out with both hands to cup them, kneading them together. Her dark hair fell over her shoulders, her wide hips surrounded me.

"Yes," she said. "Don't stop." She reached a hand between her thighs. I knew she was touching herself. She wanted to show off. She wanted to be seen. I was more than happy to watch.

"That's it," I said. "Touch your clit. Let me see you come. Pleasure yourself." I squeezed and teased breasts and nipples. I writhed underneath her, and she moved with me until finally she threw her head back and came, open-mouthed, struggling to find her breath, bright eyes shining. She was magnificent.

Tired out, she fell on top of me. I opened my arms and let her lie there while I held her tight. *Shit. I want to do everything with this woman. I want to watch her come over and over again.* But for now, I was content to listen to us both breathe into the silence of the night.

# 13. Beth

My internal alarm woke me at six a.m., which it did every morning—I rarely needed the real alarm. I hit the switch to stop it going off, slipped out of bed, collected my clothes as quietly as possible, then made for the door. I gave Chrissy one last glance before I stepped through, glad I'd oiled it because Amy complained the noise it made woke her.

In the bathroom, I used the facilities then washed and dressed. I stared at my face in the mirror while cleaning my teeth. The same old features stared out at me. *Did you expect to look different?* Daft question. Still, I often asked myself those. Didn't everyone?

Down in the kitchen, I banked up the Aga and put the kettle on. I needed a large mug of tea and my usual breakfast of toast and egg. I'd never been one for cold cereal. In deepest winter, I'd have porridge with salt, not sugar. I put the radio on to listen to the forecast.

*Damn and blast!* It seemed winter was having its final huzzah and the snow forecast for Scotland had moved south to create a mini beast from the East. I grabbed my phone and called Jed.

"I'm on my way," he said. "I've called the lads and they'll be here. I'm rounding up the sheep now to get them to milking. We can keep them in and see how bad it is. The tanker is due tomorrow so we can store today's production. Thank goodness we haven't let the lambs out yet."

"The Highland cattle will be all right and they've shelter, but we'll need to get the Herdwicks and Valois in. I'll be out there as soon as I can." I swallowed several gulps of tea and bit into the sandwich. I needed fuel on board. At least it wasn't supposed to last long. The floorboards creaked upstairs. I knew which to avoid—Chrissy didn't. I poured another mug of tea. She appeared minutes later. I didn't have time to talk about last night.

"You could have woken me" Chrissy said, wiping sleep from her eyes.

"I was about to come up." I passed her the tea. "A snow warning has been issued for this area."

"In April? This far south?"

"It happens every now and again. It seems a low-pressure system has changed its path. We had snow in June once. It's not supposed to last much more than twenty-four hours, but we have to get the animals in as close as possible to the main building It's feasible the power could go. We have a back-up generator for the milking parlour and storage. If you've got appointments today, you might want to cancel them and tell Claire to stay home. You could put something on your website."

"I will," Chrissy said. She gazed at me. "Are we all right?"

I popped two slices of bread in the toaster, then kissed the top of her head. "We're grand lass, as Ned would say. I don't have time to talk now. There's jam or eggs. Take whatever you want."

"Can I help?"

"Best not," I said, trying not to be dismissive of her offer. "We know the area and we're used to much worse. We've lost sheep in the past. They tend to shelter next to walls and get covered if the wind whips the snow into drifts."

As if to make a point the window rattled. "Stay here if you want. My computer is ready if you want to access your site. There's a spare big coat and wellies in the hall—Amy won't mind."

I finished my sandwich. "I'd better get out and sort the chickens and ducks. Animals need feeding. Come on, Ralph." The dog jumped up and wagged his tail. As I glanced outside again, the first few flakes of snow drifted down. I stood. Chrissy followed me to the door.

"Be careful out there," she said holding my arms. "I'll be fine here for now." She lifted my chin and kissed me.

"I've got to go," I said, and hurried out of the door into the cold.

Time passed in a flurry of activity and snowflakes. I sorted the fowl then checked on Geoffrey.

"Sorry, no running about in the field for you today, lad." I cleaned out the old hay and manure and spread new bedding then hung a feeding bag onto the hook, rubbed his nose then bolted the stable door. By the time I got to the milking shed, the snow had started to settle. The flakes were big, and Ralph bounced around, jumping to eat them.

"I'm glad someone's happy," I said to him. I entered through the side door. Inside, everything was as normal. I found

Jed on the walkie-talkie to his father. We couldn't depend on phones around here.

"The milkers are all accounted for. As usual, they followed us back. I think they wanted to be indoors as well. Dad's set off to round up the Herdwicks and Blacknoses, and take fodder to the cattle," he said. "Once this is done, we can herd them into the other barn. It'll be tight but we've enough fodder. I'll take Joe and fetch what we need. It shouldn't last long according to the forecast. Apparently, we're on the edge, but we all know what that can sometimes mean. I don't want to take any chances. These ladies are good milkers." He stared at me. "Good day yesterday?" he asked.

"Yes, it was." I knew what he was asking. "I left Chrissy back in the house contacting people."

He grinned. "Oh. She stopped for breakfast then."

"Yes, she did." There was no point in denying anything.

"You and I need a talk, young lady, but now is not the time."

"I'll go and help to get the barn ready for this lot." I strode back out of the door with Ralph once more at my heel. Once in the largest barn, we sorted out enclosures for the sheep. They spent a lot of the winter indoors, so were used to living this way. My phone vibrated in my pocket. I took it out. The caller didn't surprise me.

"Hi, love. Stop worrying. We're fine."

"It mentioned snow, Mum."

"There's some," I replied. "We're taking precautions. Geoffrey is safe and warm, and Ralph is with me. Most of the animals are in who need to be. Are you having fun in London?"

"I'm fine, Mum. Dad's busy, and Jenny looks like she'll give birth at any minute. I amuse myself visiting places and wandering around. And yes, I am revising as well."

The barn door opened, and sheep poured in. "I need to go, love. Sheep to deal with. Love you."

"Love you, too."

I spent the next hour helping sort out the sheep, leaving a couple of empty enclosures for the Herdwicks and Blacknoses. One of the other lads arrived with the first bunch. "A few of the Blacknoses are AWOL," he said. "Ned reckons the ewe has taken her lambs off somewhere, so he's checking. He told us to bring this lot in. You know what he's like."

I did. And I didn't like to think of him outside by himself. I found Jed in the lamb shed and explained.

"Bloody typical. He's getting too old for wandering around in snow on his own." He tried the walkie-talkie but got nothing but crackle. "Damn. Are you okay here? I'll have to go out after him."

"I know," I said. "Take care. It's easy enough to misstep in this weather." I leaned on a rail while Jed kitted himself out to face the weather then leave via the side door. All I could do now was wait. I sat on a bale of hay and took out my phone. Chrissy answered immediately.

"Are you all right?" she asked.

"I'm fine. Most of the animals are gathered up. Ned's gone off after a few Blacknoses, and Jed's gone after him."

"It's coming down a lot harder now." Chrissy sounded worried.

"Don't worry. I'm close to the house. If worse comes to worst, we have a makeshift snow plough blade we can attach to the big tractor—that'll help keep the access road open. Being on a bus route from means the big snow ploughs will come this way eventually."

"Claire said they've had some as well. I managed to put off my appointments and re-arrange them. Is there anything I can do? I feel so useless stuck in here. I could help feed a few lambs."

"I'd rather know you were safe in there. It's easy to trip in this weather." The walkie-talkie crackled into life. "I've got to go."

I pressed the button. "Beth here, over."

"Beth, it's Dad. Get the lads to come out. He's found the sheep but fallen over. I think he may have broken something. I need the stretcher. I'm okay. Hurry, please."

"Right away." He gave me their position and I shouted to the lads who sprang into action. We had a rehearsed emergency procedure. Then I rang 999 and hurried to the other barn. Chances were, we'd need to get Ned on the trailer behind the snow plough tractor to get him to the main road. I grabbed the keys from the office and set out. Twenty minutes later, we had everything ready. I jumped into the trailer, letting Joe drive the tractor. We saw three figures emerge from the snow carrying the stretcher, with the sheep and dogs preceding them. I breathed a sigh of relief and rang to check on the ambulance.

"They say they're twenty minutes away coming from the A1," I explained. "How is he?"

Ned's face appeared as white as the snow.

"He's in pain. I think he may have broken his ankle."

"Stop fussing. I'll be fine. Are those sheep in yet?" Typical Ned.

"Let's put him in the trailer and hope it's not too bumpy. We can meet the ambulance at the main gate." We placed the stretcher between bales and covered him with a blanket to try to keep Ned warm. Jed stayed with me in the trailer while Joe drove out of the yard and along the access road. We waited at the gate, hearing the sirens first then the ambulance with blue lights flashing. Jed went with his father.

"I'll call your mum and let her know. Ring when the staff tell you anything." I watched until they disappeared while Joe turned the tractor around and we headed back to the main house.

Once there, Joe jumped off the tractor. "You go in, Beth. We have all we need in the barn. We can stay overnight. I think the snow is slowing now."

It was. Reluctantly, I agreed with him. At the front door, I stomped my boots and removed my outer coat, shaking it as well before opening up. Ralph hurried in ahead of me, shaking himself in the hall. I stood in the hallway attempting to absorb heat from the radiator. Chrissy appeared with a towel.

"I think Ralph needs that more than me. Ned's had an accident. We've sent him off in an ambulance. I need to phone his wife, Daisy." Before I could say anymore arms surrounded me and pulled me close. It was wonderful to come home to someone warm.

Chrissy stroked my hair. "Come on, I'll make you a hot chocolate while you make the call."

Twenty minutes later, we were sat on the sofa with the fire blazing. Ralph lay between us with his head on my thigh. I held the mug in my hands, feeling the warmth, hoping it would spread through me.

"Is Daisy all right?" Chrissy asked.

I nodded. "She's made of Yorkshire grit. She knows Jed is there. I think she feels sorrier for the medical staff having to deal with Ned. If I know him, he'll be back at work on crutches, still bossing people around."

"Still, it must be scary. They say rain will set in tonight and it all could be gone by morning."

"We've had so much worse," Beth said. "Ned remembers the winter of 1962 when the snow lay on the ground for weeks. He made his own skis to get around. Lots of animals perished that year. I was still in London when they had it bad in 2009. Three flakes there, and the world comes to an end. Hopefully, this will be the last. We've bookings for the pods next week. Talking of which..." I didn't want to press.

"You need me out," Chrissy said. "As it happens, I had an email today saying I could move into the house next week. I've booked a removal firm to bring my stuff from home."

"I can help on the day, if you'd like me to."

"Any help gratefully received. I might need to go shopping too. I need a few things after the divorce. I know you're busy, and with Ned..."

"You know I will if I can." I yawned. I was tired to my bones. I reached out my hand over a sleeping Ralph. "Would you like to stay over again? I can't send you out in the dark, and I don't want to."

Chrissy gazed at me. "I'd love to stay."

"I'm not sure I'm up to anything amorous. It's been a long day."

"Cuddling it is then."

Ralph shifted, snored, then let out a huge fart. Chrissy shoved the cushion against his arse, and we laughed.

"I'm glad you're here," I said.

It was good not to be alone.

# 14. Chrissy

The snow was gone in no time. After two days, only a few white patches lingered against stone walls, and a week later the sun was shining with real warmth—Britain didn't have a climate, just every weather possible and often on the same day. Easter weekend had passed, the new lambs were all out in the fields, and two new Highland cow calves had been born—they were so cute.

I'd been busy with the bridal shop and with organising everything to do with the move. I had the keys to the house and tomorrow was moving day. Beth had also been busy with Ned being out of action. He'd broken his ankle in two places, and although he was back home, his wife had put her foot down— no attempting to organise sheep on crutches. Instead, she'd taken him to their daughter's bungalow in York to rest up, be spoilt, and spend time with his grandson. Amy had returned early from London to help. Beth and I had had little time to talk, and I hoped she wasn't regretting everything and avoiding me. Yes, paranoia and doubt occupied much of my thoughts.

We'd been busy over the Easter weekend. As usual, as many bank holidays were used as an excuse to shop. I did stay closed on Sunday but spent the day at the new house cleaning and measuring, making lists of what I'd need. Today, Easter Monday, Claire and I had assisted three brides to find their perfect look. It never got boring hearing a bride-to-be use the word beautiful to describe herself. Today, there had been tears more than once—but happy tears—the best sort.

"After tomorrow, I'll be able to pick you up and drop you home every day," I said, as we packed everything away for the night.

"Are you sure you don't need any help?" she asked.

"No, I'll be fine. You work long hours and weekends with me already, Claire. Have a day out. The forecast is great. Enjoy it before you're back here."

She gazed at me. "You know I love this job, don't you? I've learnt so much, and it's helped me to feel better about myself, that maybe, there is someone out in the big wide world for me. I'm not good with people. I don't trust easily. I helped out at the inn yesterday, and this bloke asked me out. I thought he was joking, but turned out he was serious. He's a district nurse and has recently moved into the area. I've chatted to him a few times over the bar."

I sat on the edge of my desk. "What did you say?"

"I said I'd call him. He has the afternoon off tomorrow, and you said I could have the afternoon off... He's new to the area and hasn't been to York. I could show him the sights. Is taking someone to the Minster anyone's idea of a date?"

"Well, I'd like to go," I said. "Or you could always go to the coast. Ring him and see. I've updated the website about opening hours. And you never know, he might be your perfect person." A car horn sounded outside.

"That's my lift. Mum will be glad she doesn't have to bother again. Have a good day tomorrow."

"You, too."

I finished tidying then switched off and locked up before making my way over to the pod. The Highland cows were in the field. I enjoyed the warmth of the sun and stared at them for a while. I was already packed. I planned an evening of a microwaved ready meal and a soak in the hot tub while I still had one. I'd miss it. I'd miss being on the farm. I reluctantly left the cows as they wandered off and back at the pod, ate a lasagne while watching the latest episode of *Doctor Who*.

A knock on the door made me pause. I stood to open it and found Beth on the veranda.

"I thought I'd come and check you were all right and ready for the move tomorrow."

"I think so. I'm packed here and hopefully the traffic will be in my favour and the removal men will get to the house on time. Do you want to come in." I was conscious we both might feel awkward. I stood back and followed Beth in.

"I didn't know you were into *Doctor Who*. I've never watched it. I'm more of a political or crime drama fan."

I paused the TV. "So I saw from your DVD collection. Me and Rob have been fans since the new ones began. He goes to conventions as well, but he's more of a general nerdy geek than me. Sit down. D'you want a drink? I was about to make coffee."

"Thanks. If it's no bother."

I made us a mug each and sat on the bed opposite her. I wasn't sure what to say so I waited.

"I'm sorry I haven't seen you last week. I wasn't deliberately avoiding you or anything. With Ned out of action we've been busy, and the vet has been doing health checks on the sheep and new lambs. We have to keep a constant eye out for mastitis. It can cause massive problems in a flock. And with Amy returning early, it's been difficult to—"

"It's okay," I said, as she spoke faster and faster. "I know how busy you are. I've been busy myself. You don't owe me an explanation." I waited as some of the tension eased out of her.

"I didn't want you to think." She paused. "Oh fuck. I didn't want you to think or not think—I don't know. What happened is a bit mind-boggling for me. You know I've never—"

"Slept with a woman."

"Well, yes. But there's more. Bloody hell. I wish we were having this conversation in the dark. I mean. I like you, and I liked what we did. I'd like to do it again, but I don't know if I can. I don't know if I'm ready to be someone different."

"*Would* you be different?" I asked.

Beth picked up her mug and took several mouthfuls. "I feel like I would be. Until last week, I was Beth Nethering, a divorcee with a teenage daughter who owns this farm which has been in the family for hundreds of years, was a successful lawyer, and hadn't had sex for ten years."

"And aren't you still most of those things?"

"Yes, I suppose I am, but now it's like I'm seeing things in a different way, like if I'd got new glasses, but instead of everything being clearer, things are more complex."

"Look, Beth. I like you. I think we could be great friends, but I find you attractive as well. I'm not going to deny, I want to sleep with you again, but I'm newly divorced myself, and I'm not sure what I'm ready for yet. I've a new business, and I'm moving tomorrow. I don't need any more stress. If we enjoy each other, it's not a lifetime commitment—not yet anyway. Are you worried people will talk because you're friendly with the lesbian dress seller?"

Her cheeks turned red, and I knew I'd hit home. "Karen asked me to come for dinner. I've put her off, but she can be like a dog with a bone at times."

"Who you tell is up to you. I'll tell Rob. It's hard to keep stuff from him. I was stupid when I got married and let Molly control so many aspects of our life together. I didn't realise I'd lost a lot of my university friends until the relationship fell apart. Our friends were really her friends. But I always had Rob. She couldn't shake him off. So I could do with more friends. It's partly why I came here—to start again and join in a few local activities, meet new people."

Beth hummed. "I know a lot of people. I lost friends when I went to university, and then lost those when I came back. I have Jed and Karen, and others who know me. And there's Amy. My daughter has grown into a caring person, and she loves the farm."

"Which is down to you. But she'll be away in less than a year."

"She intends to come back. But I know anything could happen. As long as *we're* all right."

"We are." I had some niggling worries, but I wasn't intending to share.

"Tomorrow," she said. "Amy is revising with one of her school friends all day and staying overnight. She's riding Geoffrey over. I suspect they'll do more riding than revising, but that's good for her. I thought you might like my help opening boxes and sorting furniture."

"I'd love it. I've new sofas arriving in the morning, but I don't expect the removal van until midday. They're collecting everything out of storage first."

"I'll bring lunch over," Beth said. "I need to get off now and put the chooks and ducks to bed. Up before dawn in the morning."

"And tonight, I intend to have my last stint in the hot tub while I can then get an early night." I stood as she did, so we were inches away from each other.

"I'll see you tomorrow," I said.

She moved first. I stopped at the door.

"I'm glad I came over."

"Me too," I replied. I watched her go along the path then turned back into the pod. Time for one last soak.

The next day, I was out before eight. Claire would call if she felt out of her depth should anyone arrive without an appointment in the morning. I sat in my car and started the engine. It wasn't as if I was leaving the place entirely. Now, I had a new home to look forward to, one, which although it wasn't my own, I could furnish as I wanted.

I reached the property thirty minutes later. On the outside, the house was older and part of a terrace. It was double-fronted and built of stone with two large rooms downstairs running front to back. To the left, as I walked through the door, was the living room with a window at the front and French windows looking out on the small, paved courtyard. Behind this was a garage but no designated parking—today I parked on the green at the front and hoped the various delivery and removal vans would find enough space while people were out at work for the day.

To the right was a kitchen/diner. The units were Shaker

style, painted beige with beech worktops and a Belfast sink. For now, I left my suitcases at the bottom of the stairs and walked into the living room. I sat on the hardwood floor and tried to imagine placing the furniture I'd bought. Picking myself up, I wandered through to the outside. Maybe I could get pots and cheer the space up and set up bird feeders. I'd need to buy a bench to sit on. I returned inside. The doorbell rang, then the door opened.

"Hello. It's Beth."

"I'm in the kitchen to the right," I called out. The door pushed open, and Beth walked in carrying bags.

"I come bearing gifts of food, crockery, and cutlery. I know from experience you always find them in the last box you open. And I've bought a kettle as well. We'll need a mug of tea at some point." She turned taking in the space.

"It's nicely done out, isn't it? Although, beige is dull. You'll be able to add your own touches. I'll put this lot away and make us a cuppa, shall I?"

"That would be great. I'm sorry there's nowhere to sit yet. Did you manage to park?"

"I'm right behind you. Don't worry, there's still plenty of space out there. Moving is such a faff, especially when you're trying to co-ordinate deliveries. And there's the van now. Where do you want me? I can stay in here and make tea. I brought a couple of mugs."

"Sounds good. I'll go and direct everything to the right room." I hurried to the front door. The men were already opening the back of the truck.

"Ms Wychling?" one of them asked.

"That's me," I said.

"Just tell us where you want everything, and we'll be on our way. Sofas first."

The delivery went smoothly. Sofas into the living room, table and chairs into the dining room, divan, and mattress, along with numerous flat pack boxes in the main bedroom.

"Sign here, please." I signed his form, took the receipt, and hoped a tenner each was enough. I was grateful not to have to take all those heavy boxes upstairs. Beth handed me a new brew.

"The other went cold." She pulled out a still wrapped chair and sat. I joined her.

"How are your flatpack building skills?" I said.

"Funny you should ask. I brought my toolkit just in case. A farmer has to be able to turn her hand to anything and you never know when an electric screwdriver will come in handy."

I grinned. "I thought we might unwrap the table and chairs first then have a go at the wardrobe as it's the biggest item. At least the bed is made, and they took away all the plastic wrapping. And now, I'll have somewhere to sit and somewhere to lie down."

Beth gazed straight at me from under her fringe. "The bed looks roomy and comfortable."

I held her gaze. "I like a big bed. It gives me room to move around if I need it."

"I noticed this place has a decent-sized bath too. It's not quite a hot tub but at least you'll have somewhere to relax after a long day of furniture-building and unpacking."

I finished the coffee and placed the mug on the table. "That, my friend, is an excellent point."

Constructing the wardrobe turned out to be easier than I expected. The bedroom was big enough to give us space and we soon had it built and against the wall. My biggest worry was not scratching the highly polished wooden floor. Next, we tackled the chest of drawers, followed by the dressing table and bedside table. The stuff wasn't finest oak, but it seemed all right in situ.

"A van has pulled up," Beth said from the window seat. "Timed that nicely. I suggest getting everything in then having lunch. I'm famished. Remember my day began at six."

I prayed all the right labels had been placed on the right boxes. I directed the furniture I'd brought from my old house to the new rooms—there wasn't much. I'd also kept three hanging racks which could be stored in the spare bedroom. In the end it didn't take long. I sat on a sofa with Beth and stared at a wall of boxes. The last time I'd had one was when I'd moved in with Molly.

"You okay?" Beth asked clearly catching my mood. "Moving is stressful at any time. I remember packing away my stuff. Luckily, Graham and I didn't argue, and the farmhouse had furniture already. Neil hadn't changed anything, but over the years, I've made a few additions. A new bed was my first priority. It seemed wrong enough sleep in my parents' room without knowing I was sleeping where I'd been conceived—the bed was that old."

I sighed and glanced around. "It seems strange I'm going to be living here. Being in the pod was like being on an extended holiday. It'll be many months before I can think about buying a place, so this is my home for now."

"It's a nice home. And the town is lovely. There's a few decent little shops, including I noticed a chippy, and some beautiful walks nearby along the river. I wonder what the neighbours are like."

"I'm hoping for a deaf old lady who makes cakes not a bloke

with a big car who is lousy at parking and loves hip-hop. Now, you mentioned food."

We ate a gorgeous range of deli products washed down with homemade fizzy lemonade then began on the kitchen boxes. Bit by bit, every box was opened and kitchen equipment, unwrapped, checked, and put away. By late afternoon, we'd finished downstairs. Only the contents of the bedroom boxes needed emptying, and they could wait for now.

"As we've discovered there is a local chip shop here. How about I treat you to a fish and chip tea?"

"Sounds marvellous. I can't remember when I last had one. I'll have mushy peas as well but no salt or vinegar."

Beth stared at me. "Really? Oh well, each to their own. I'll see what fish they have. I could do with a stroll."

While she was gone, I scooted upstairs, found the bedding box, and made the bed, proud I'd managed to put on the duvet cover on my own. The bright yellow flowers cheered up the room and didn't clash with the green curtains. I also located the box with the towels, which might come in handy later. I planned to play the evening by ear and see how things worked out. Suggestions were one thing, and cold feet were another. While upstairs, I checked on Claire and hoped I wasn't interrupting anything.

"Hi, Chrissy. Everything okay?" Claire sounded bright.

"Amazingly, everything went to plan. Beth has gone to get us fish and chips. How's today been for you?" I suspected from her voice she had something to tell me.

"I sold a dress this morning," she said. "Oh, it was lovely. Selling dresses makes me so happy?"

I didn't interrupt. I knew that joy.

"This woman came in with her sister. Her size was at the

top end of our lines, and she was so sad. She had this dress, but it wasn't a real wedding dress, and the wedding is Saturday. Her sister saw our advert in the *Post* and persuaded her to come. I showed her the strapless design with the corseting and the bling set just below the waist. You know the one with the longer train?"

"I do."

"She wouldn't believe she could wear it, but with her sister's help we got everything pulled in. We set her hair, found a tiara and beautiful ivory lace veil. Honestly, I cried. She looked glorious. And her face when she saw herself in the mirror. I think we used a whole box of tissues for those tears of joy. Long story short. She bought it and asked me if I could help her get dressed at the wedding. Her mother died when she was little and left her this beautiful amethyst necklace. I found a tiara with purple stones too. So am I all right to take Saturday off?"

"You'll be working so of course I'll pay you," I said. "And congratulations. How's the date going?"

"Wonderfully, Matt is lovely, really lovely. We went round the Minster and had afternoon tea in one of those little cafes. He's on call for emergencies this evening, but he wants to meet me again. We had such a lot in common."

"That's wonderful." I replied. "I've got to go now. Don't forgot I'll pick you up at eight-thirty tomorrow. Bye now." I slipped the phone into my pocket.

"Claire sounded excited" Beth said. I hadn't noticed her standing there.

"She sold a dress. It doesn't sound a lot when you say it, but it was. And her date with Matt, the district nurse went well. She deserves some fun.

"She does. And I told you, she loves this job. Now, the food is getting cold. Care to join me for gourmet haddock and chips with mushy peas accompanied by dandelion and burdock?"

"Dandelion and what?" I asked.

Beth stared at me. "You've never had it? Just you wait. It's a taste sensation."

It turned out I liked the sweet stuff, and the food. We sat on a sofa with our feet up and ate our meals from the newspaper with our fingers. Every time Beth licked them, something in my stomach did the hokey-cokey but in a good way. The room quickly acquired a lived-in smell. I made a mental note to buy scented candles.

Beth scrunched her food wrappers. "I'll make tea." She took my wrappers off me, and I lay back with my feet on my coffee table. The rays of the setting sun streamed in through the windows behind me, giving the room a warm glow. Beth returned with the mugs of tea.

"Having a loo under the stairs is useful," she said, turning around. "I like this place. I wonder if the owner would sell. You could be cosy here." She sat next to me.

"It's a thought," I said. We sat for a moment staring out through the French windows at the other end of the room. I wanted to ask her to stay over. I wanted to ask her about that bath, but fear got the better of me.

"I think I could do with a bath and an early night." Beth murmured while staring ahead. Had she read my mind?

"I'd love one," I replied. "I found the towels and bubble bath." I grabbed the arm of the sofa to stop my hand from trembling.

"The hot water is working," she said. "I checked."

"That's good. Do you want to go upstairs now while I switch off here?"

"I'll start running the bath then."

She stood, turned slightly, and held out a hand. A slight smile crossed her lips. "If it's any help, I'm more than a little terrified too. Silly, isn't it? We're both grown-ups. Don't be long."

She left the room. I locked up, and switched off, then followed her.

# 15. Beth

Once upstairs, I ran a bath and lit the four scented candles I'd included in among the food supplies I'd brought. I found the bubble bath, then stripped off and climbed in. All the while, I asked myself the same questions over and over. *Do you know what you're doing? Answer no. Are you out of your tiny mind? Maybe. Do you care? Not enough.* The water was warm and soothing after such a busy day. I lay with my head back, splashing gently with my hands to increase the bubbly coverage and waited for Chrissy to appear.

After a few minutes, footsteps echoed on the wooden stairs. Despite the warmth of the water, I shivered with anticipation. I'd never shared a bath with anyone in my whole life—not even my husband. We hadn't had shower sex either. We tried once, but discovered it wasn't as simple as it always sounded in books or appeared on films. The door opened and Chrissy walked in, wrapped in a jade-green towel.

"This is lovely," she said. "You came prepared, I see." Heat rushed into my face, and I knew I was blushing madly.

"I'll turn off the light then get in and sit front of you."

She moved quickly and settled herself between my thighs with her back to me. I sat up enough to kiss the back of her neck.

"Hmm, this is soothing." She eased herself back until she lay with her head almost between my breasts. "A bath was a good idea after such a busy day." She reached for a sponge and body wash.

"Here, let me," I said. I squeezed out the gel, making lather, then rubbed the sponge over her shoulders, chest, and arms. So many smells hit my senses from the candles, the bubbles, and the body wash. Chrissy took the sponge from me and washed the rest of her body. We didn't talk. The only sound was the drip of water as some escaped over the side onto the bathmat.

"Sit, and I'll do your back," I said when she'd finished. Again, I moved the sponge in circles, covering all areas. Chrissy made small moaning sounds. Finally, I stopped washing, placed a palm on each shoulder, and massaged them gently.

"You have great hands," she said.

"Must be handling all those sheep," I replied.

"All I can say, is lucky sheep."

"D'you want me to wash your hair?" Even considering our current positions and what we'd done before, this seemed more intimate.

"Please. The gel can also be used for hair, and I put a cup on the side."

I washed it like I'd done many times for Amy when she was little, though with less screaming about soap getting into eyes. Finally, as the bubbles were fading, I rinsed then grabbed a towel to rub her head dry.

"Time to get out," she said, then eased herself up.

I thought I should look away as she shook out her hair, but I didn't. Instead, I stared at her long limbs and perfect breasts. Instinctively, I covered mine. She wrapped her robe around herself.

"I'll see you in the bedroom. There's a towel out ready for you."

I gave myself a quick wash then exited the bath. I found Chrissy sitting on the edge of her bed, blow-drying her hair, still wearing her robe, and I sat next to her.

"This towel is luxuriously fluffy," I said, pulling it round me once more. I gazed at Chrisy in the mirror. She held herself so well with her body straight and her shoulders back. Chrissy wouldn't ever be called conventionally pretty, but she was gorgeous with her thick, blonde hair, usually held in an untidy bun or ponytail, now cascading over her shoulders. I'd always loved the colour of my hair, dark like my father's had been, with a tendency to curl. I suspected, like him, I'd end up going grey before I was sixty. I was determined to do it gracefully.

The noise stopped. "Are you all right?" I realised Chrissy was talking to me. Well, there was no one else.

"Yeah, sorry just thinking. What did you say?"

"It doesn't matter."

I glanced at the clock on the bedside table. "I'll need to put an alarm on for five-thirty to get back to the farm in the morning. Sorry about that."

"I thought you would. It's not late now," Chrissy said. "Do you want to get into bed?"

Instinctively, I pulled the towel tighter around me. "I'm sorry. I'm still not comfortable being naked under bright lights, especially in front of a mirror."

Chrissy reached over and dimmed the lights. "Is that better? You know you have nothing to worry about." She placed her hand where the fabric overlapped.

"Can I?"

I nodded. Words refused to form. She tugged at the cloth, slowly exposing me. Without warning, she stood, let the robe fall from her body, then knelt between my legs. *Shit!* My senses reeled. I could smell the body wash on her hair and hear our breathing. My heartrate rocketed and I gasped for air. I stared into the mirror as she swayed forward and captured one of my nipples between her lips. She sucked hard. I let my head fall back. I wanted to watch but found I couldn't. Now, all I wanted to do was *feel*. She moved from one nipple to another, licking, sucking, and gently nipping at them with her teeth. Damp poured out of me and I worried about the sheet underneath me. She stopped.

"Why don't you get into bed?"

I sat straight. Chrissy ran her tongue over her lips and smiled at me.

"You're skilled at that," I said.

"I'm skilled at lots of things. And now I want you on your back with my face buried between your thighs."

*Fucking hell. How do people just say those things out loud?* I didn't ask. Instead, I did as I was instructed, placing my head on the pillow, and staring at the ceiling. Chrissy moved to the bottom of the bed and gently parted my legs. At least I was clean and not sweaty. She edged up the mattress getting closer and closer. I raised my hips in anticipation of contact. Would she lick me? Suck me? Fuck me? Would I come? Would it be the same?

"Draw up your knees." Her hot breath hit my skin, then

fingers exposed my clit, and finally I felt the touch of her tongue as she buried her face in my pussy. She pressed and teased, and I gasped. This felt nothing like a hard vibrator. She changed from lapping at the area with the whole surface to using the tip to touch the exact spot I needed. Though she concentrated on my clit, a feeling grew inside me, demanding to be let out. My muscles tightened, and I grabbed the sheet.

"Don't stop," I whispered. "Please, don't stop." The second was more of a desperate plea.

She didn't. Two fingers slipped inside me. My climax gathered and gathered, but I wanted this sensation to last forever. I wanted to come, but I didn't want it at the same time, because then this sensation would be over. In the end, my body made its choice. I tensed in anticipation, which pulled me away from her. She followed and licked harder until my body exploded.

"Oh hell, you are incredible." She continued until I could take no more and I touched her head. "Please, I can't."

She stopped, lifted herself so she knelt between my legs, licked her lips, then smiled at me. I should have felt embarrassed and exposed, but I didn't. I wanted her to see me, the woman she'd given such pleasure to.

"Bloody hell, Beth, but you're beautiful."

"Thank you." I accepted the compliment. "Lie next to me."

She shifted and tucked herself under my arm with her head resting on my breast. I leaned forward to kiss her, tasting myself on her lips. I reached my hand lower. *I'm so wet.*

"What do you need?" I asked. Truth was I was knackered. I'd worried about this—not coming at the same time—not that I had often with Graham.

"Touch me," she said.

I turned onto my side and reached between her legs. She too was damp. I reached out a finger, found the spot I wanted, and pressed in a circular movement. As I did, I sucked on her nipple and threw my arm across her body. She groaned and I pressed harder.

"Close now," she said. "Won't take long." She arched her back and let out a cry saying my name. I slowed, then stopped and pulled her close.

"Thank you. I needed that." She yawned. I followed suit.

"Sleep now," I said.

She turned and I spooned behind her.

"You're so lovely," she whispered and pulled my arm around her. I was too tired for thoughts I didn't want to have regrets. I didn't want to fear. For now, I had my lover wrapped in my arms. Sleep claimed me minutes later.

I woke the next morning with the alarm, realising I had two immediate problems. The first was an urgent need for the loo. The second was I'd left my clothes folded on the chest of drawers at the other side of the room. Fortunately, Chrissy only shifted slightly and groaned before burying herself back under the duvet, and with it being half-past five, it was still dark. I slipped out from the bed, scurried across the room, grabbed my clothes, and hurried to the bathroom. Fifteen minutes later, I was dressed and ready to head off home.

Back in the bedroom, Chrissy had turned over and opened her eyes when I came in. I sat on the side of the bed.

"Sorry, I've got to go. The farm starts early, and I've animals to feed and clean out." Also, I knew Jed would be around getting the sheep in for milking. For sure, he'd notice my car was missing and launch a Spanish-style inquisition to determine if I'd stayed out overnight.

Chrissy squinted at me. "Are we all right?" she asked.

"Yes." I whispered. "I don't want to announce anything to the world, but last night was…" I searched for a word. Last night had been so many things, both scary and exciting. "Last night was lovely." I leaned over and kissed her lips and was rewarded with a smile. We needed to talk. Of course we needed to talk, but now wasn't the time.

"Got to go."

Outside, I locked the door and put the key back through the letterbox. There was a nip in the air when I got to my car and hints of daylight had begun to send streaks of colour across the sky. I turned on the engine and the radio. I wasn't ready for thought as I drove along the country roads, so I sang along with the music and listened to the news, hoping the government wouldn't announce anything to make my life more difficult. Minutes before seven, I pulled into the yard in front of the main house. Hopefully, I'd achieved my aim. Once in, I fed a starving dog and rushed upstairs to wash, change, and clean my teeth. I made a mug of tea in my reusable cup and grabbed a couple of pieces of toast. I could have more later.

Once outside, I began the day with my usual chores. First came the chickens and ducks. I fed them and collected the eggs then headed for the stables. After I got there, I remembered Geoffrey was with Amy. I cleaned out his stall and fed the two farm cats who strolled in. Misty and Feisty were rescues who did an excellent job of keeping the vermin population under control, even if they did sometimes leave presents on the doorstep. They chose to live outside in all weathers but weren't averse to a cuddle.

Outside again, the lambs were out in the fields, and the ewes had been called in. They followed Jed or his father as if they were following the Pied Piper, leaving the dogs little work to do. I decided to leave the milking alone. Today was an admin day. I had a lot to do, and a meeting later to seal the contracts to create the ice cream production part of the company. So much of this job was paperwork, but fine detail was my strength and I often advised others on legal issues. It brought in extra income and meant I kept my legal brain both working and up-to-date.

Finally, I checked on the glamping pods. Two had been occupied over the Easter weekend. Mary was cleaning and getting things ready for the next visitors. Over the fence the cows grazed on fodder one of the lads had brought in. After a quick word, I headed back to the house. This was my day. This was my life. The sound of a car and voices nearby told me Chrissy and Claire had arrived to start *their* day.

The sun emerged from behind a cloud and warmth hit my back. I picked up the basket of eggs on the step. Jed appeared without warning.

"Using your ninja stealth powers again," I said.

"Good night?" he asked grinning.

"Haven't you got something to do?" I replied. Ralph barked from behind the door.

"I thought I'd take Ralph out with these two as Amy isn't here. Joe and the lads have everything in hand with the sheep, and the lambs are out."

"Please. He needs a run. I've got mountains of paperwork to deal with, and I've no idea when Amy will show her face. I opened the door and Jed whistled. Ralph scrambled to his feet and stood, tongue lolling.

"Beth."

"Yes," I said turning to face him.

"You know where I am if you need to talk."

I nodded. "Thank you." I stepped inside and closed the door behind me then leaned against it. I needed to block out the swirling mess in my brain. I strode forward until I reached my desk and began to work my way through the piles of papers.

# 16. Chrissy

As I drove to collect Claire, the sun was shining, and the birds were singing. I'd even watched a squirrel scampering across the green before I'd set off. After yesterday, I should have been grinning and full of the joys of spring, and yet, I wasn't. Doom and gloom and a nasty case of the what-ifs had set in as soon as I'd heard Beth close the front door. Yes, a secret affair could be exciting, but it could also be heartbreaking. I could tell myself this was a bit of fun. I could tell myself all sorts of things, and usually did. It didn't matter how many times my brain made me work out those what- ifs, it had a habit of turning itself into a multi-verse—if A happens does it lead to disaster, or if B happens will we live happy ever after, all the way through to if Z happens. I wasn't keen on surprises. Despite never being a scout, I liked to be prepared.

I drove to the car park at the back of the White Hart, took out my phone and texted Claire I'd arrived. If I'd been more observant, I'd have noticed a familiar car, but my mind was too occupied with other things. When Claire stepped out of the rear door she was not alone. With her stood my parents, and

Rob and Ingrid. I experienced a feeling somewhere between joy and pure panic. I got out of the car, rushed towards them, and was enveloped in the family hug.

"How are you here?" I asked.

"The usual way," my father replied. "Via the M25 and M1. We thought we'd surprise you. Your mother was worried."

"No I wasn't, darling. Take no notice. Your father, on the other hand. You know what he's like. You're still his little girl, and you've been through such a lot. And let's face it, you're here surrounded by strangers."

I smiled at Claire and shrugged. "And you decided to come along for the ride," I said to Rob.

"Well, we didn't get a honeymoon, so we've a couple of nights here with Mum and Dad and then we're off to Edinburgh. We're keeping the car and Mum and Dad are going home by train on Friday. Ingrid is desperate to see the shop."

"I am. And the farm with the animals, and your new house. It's all so exciting. Claire has filled us in on some things. She and her family have been so helpful, and it's a lovely place—such a pretty village. We had a walk around last night before it got too dark. And the food was excellent."

"And the prices," my father exclaimed. "I couldn't believe how much cheaper a pint was compared to the south. Not to mention your mother's favourite tipple. She even got squiffy."

My mother frowned. "I did not. Don't believe a words he says."

"Hmm," I said, not really listening. "Well, as you are here, I suppose you'd better follow us to the shop. We've appointments this afternoon, but sometimes people just turn up, like you lot."

Rob strolled to my car. "Why don't me and Ingrid come

with you, and Claire can travel with Mum and Dad, just in case. It's easy to get lost on country roads."

"I can do that," Claire said helpfully.

I knew Rob would have an ulterior motive. We settled ourselves into the cars. I'd hardly got out of the village before the first question.

"So," he said. "Beth sounds interesting. Karen at the hotel mentioned you'd been spending time with her.

"She's my landlord," I answered too quickly and definitely too defensively.

"Hmm."

I glanced at the rear-view mirror to see his smiling face. *Smarmy bastard.*

"I believe she helped you move into your new house yesterday. That was kind of her. It's good you're making friends."

If Ingrid hadn't been there, we'd have ended up having a heated discussion. Instead, I pointed out a few landmarks and features along the way. I already knew this would end with me spilling the beans. We'd never been able to keep secrets from each other, and he'd always been my best friend as well as my brother.

"And here we are," I said, pointing to the sign I'd had put up.

"I love the name," Ingrid said. "It makes me happy to know all these women are getting the same help I did to be awesome on their big day. It must be so satisfying for you too." My sister-in-law had always had the ability to change the subject in a positive way.

"It is. So far, I love it here, and Claire has been a Godsend. We sold a dress to a minor member of the aristocracy a few weeks back. Word of mouth is what we need. But we've also someone booked to come from Scotland the first week in May. We've had features in local papers, and soon we've got an interview and picture spread with *Yorkshire Brides Monthly Magazine*."

"Are those Highland cows?" Rob asked. "They're far from home down here."

"Beth keeps a few. Her dad bred them. There are cute sheep too, as well as the milkers."

"Milking sheep is different, isn't?" Ingrid said.

"Maybe in Britain, but there's lots in Europe. Beth says the milk has certain properties. I get lost in the science. They sell the milk and make cheese and yoghurt. Their next venture is making ice cream. Beth is part of a group of local producers who joined together."

I pulled into the car park. "And here we are."

"It's bigger than I expected," Rob said. "Looks good though."

We stepped out of the car as the others arrived. My parents strolled over, taking everything in.

"You can't smell the farm," Mum said. "I thought it would be off-putting. The premises are great. The views are lovely. I can hear the birds singing. You wouldn't get all this on a high street."

Claire had already opened up, so we followed her into the showing area. Dad sat to rest his plumber's knees, as he called them, while Mum examined the dresses on display. *I need more photographs*. Perhaps, I could persuade Ingrid to model for me, along with Claire, who emerged with a tray of coffees and placed them on the table.

"This is where the supporters sit and the bride comes in to

show them the dresses," Claire explained. "We have catalogues for them to look through, which helps us to work out what they want, or think they want. Chrissy is brilliant with them—building their confidence. So many have come to us completely disheartened, and we find them something. There's so much to this job, but what I love the most is making people happy. Would you like to see the dress collection, Mrs Wychling?"

"Yes, please." My mother and Ingrid replied at the same time. "And do call me Yvonne," my mother said. "To avoid any confusion."

I left Claire to it. I could hear her explaining the layout, and about some of our clients. I sat with Dad and Rob.

"How's the finances, love?" Dad being self-employed, knew the pitfalls.

"Beth's ex-husband is an accountant and has agreed to take on my books. He does the farm. And Beth is a lawyer, so she's volunteered to help with any new contracts."

"Convenient," Rob said.

"Yes, isn't it?" I glared at him.

"Do you think she'd let us have a tour around the farm?" Dad asked.

"I can ask. You have to take care though." I took out my phone.

*Hi. Surprise visit from my family. They would like to see the farm. We are at the shop now. I'll make sure they are careful.*

The reply came straight away.

*I could do with a break from paperwork. Give me 30 mins and I'll meet you at the farmhouse door. Good thing they didn't visit the house last night.*

Heat rushed into my face. I didn't want to think about that possibility. Having Beth meet my family was terrifying enough.

"Okay. Beth says she'll meet us. I'll take you there after we've finished the coffees." Claire returned with my mother and Ingrid.

"Take all the time you like," Claire said. "I can stay with Ingrid and Yvonne. We can have fun checking out the dresses or maybe stroll down to see the Highland cows."

My mother patted Claire's arm. "Russ wants to see all the machinery, and I have no interest."

"I'll come back here and meet you," I said.

Later, once outside, Dad dug into the boot of his car and pulled out two pairs of wellies. "We came prepared," he said, brandishing them with a flourish. "Now, lead on."

Rob grinned. There was mischief in his eyes.

Beth met us on the doorstep. Amy stood with her, accompanied by Ralph.

"Amy said she'd been happy to have a break from revision and show your father and brother around the place. I've got an online meeting in twenty minutes to discuss ice cream."

"I'm Beth's daughter," Amy said. "And this is Ralph. I'm glad you brought your wellies. It's muddy this morning. I rode back from a friend's house earlier on. Now, shall we start in the lambing barns? We've still a few being hand-fed."

I waited while Amy led them off chatting away, then turned back to Beth.

"Come in for a minute," she said.

I followed her into the kitchen desperate to kiss her—to reconnect in some way. Instead, she kissed me, pushing me against a wall. After my mouth, she kissed my jawline, and my neck. Her hands roamed my body seeking access under my jumper. "Do you really have a meeting?" I asked between breaths.

"Sadly, I do. I wanted you not to feel awkward." She stopped and stepped back. "We're all right, aren't we?"

"Yes," I mumbled. Not at all sure of my words.

"It must have been a shock—your family turning up without warning."

"It was, I can tell you. I think Rob has suspicions about us. He knows me too well. Apparently, he was talking to Karen last night. Have you said anything to her?"

"No, not her. Jed knows some. He won't say anything."

"I'd better get back to Mum and Ingrid. We're going to take photographs of Claire and Ingrid in dresses to put on the shop walls. I wondered if you'd be willing to do some."

"Me? Really?"

"Yes, with your build and colouring, you'd be perfect. I could do your hair and make-up. Haven't you ever played dress-up?"

Her cheeks reddened.

"You've a story, haven't you?"

Beth glanced at her watch. "I must go. I need to collect my information for this meeting. We can talk later." She kissed my cheek and gave me a quick hug.

Back at the bridal barn, I found Claire taking photographs of Ingrid with my mother choosing the dresses. I remembered the bride who'd come to me in tears. The joy on her face as she posed for the camera was what made this choice of mine worthwhile.

The outside bell rang, telling me we had visitors. The inner door opened, and a woman stepped through followed by two men, which was unusual in itself. The woman's gaze darted around the room. She was like a rabbit in headlights, clearly terrified. She half-turned, but one of the men held her arms.

"Come on, sis. We're here with you. Daz would be here too if you'd let him. You know how much he loves you. He'll do whatever you want for your big day. Remember, when you were little, you always wanted the works, and the big dress."

I stepped forward. "Hi, my name is Chrissy. I'm here to help. Sorry, we were taking photographs for publicity. That's my mum and sister-in-law with my assistant Claire."

Ingrid, who was wearing a strapless dress, with a corseted bodice and wide skirt covered with patterned lace and crystals, turned to face us. She crossed the room and took hold of the woman's hands. Bloody hell, my brother had been so lucky to find this woman.

"I know it seems scary, and I don't know what you've been through, but Chrissy and Claire will help you. Chrissy helped me find my perfect dress. Mum, pass my bag, will you?" She rummaged inside and took out her phone.

"Here," she said, after pressing a few buttons. "This is me and my husband on our wedding day."

"You look beautiful." Tears slipped from our visitor's eyes and over her cheeks.

Her brother wrapped his arms around her from behind then glanced at me. "Hi, this is my sister, Gracie. I'm Huw, and this is my husband, Dominic. We're here for moral support."

"It's lovely to meet you. Shall we sit down, and we can talk about what sort of dress you want." I grabbed my sketch pad.

"I'll get changed," Ingrid said. "Then we'll stroll down to the field."

"No, please. Could you stay? These two are great, but I don't have a sister, or a mum, and my best friend had to work. We've come from Oswestry yesterday. Dom saw something about you online."

"We'd be happy to help," Mum said.

We talked. As was common, Gracie talked about covering herself. I asked if she'd let us choose something. The worst thing in these circumstances was someone choosing a dress that wouldn't fit. I knew what would, but I also knew Gracie wouldn't choose it for herself in a month of Sundays.

"Okay, why don't you come through to the back and we'll try a few on. I think I have the perfect dress to suit you."

I got Gracie to put on a robe then close her eyes as she stepped into the dress. Claire and I pulled it over her hips. The full skirt had layers topped by lace with tiny flowers. A circle of crystals could sit on her hips or waist. Claire and I pulled the laces at the back of the corseted bodice helping to create a shape and not the blob—Gracie's word—she feared.

"I'm too big for it, aren't I," Grace said.

"No. It fits you perfectly. Keep your eyes closed." I made sure the back was high enough to cover any of the bulges Grace feared, then attached a lace shoulder covering that fitted over the top of the arm. Claire passed me a headband and long veil without prompting.

"Now, we're going to lead you out to show the others. Keep your eyes closed. There's a step to the podium."

"Close your eyes, everyone," Claire warned.

We led Gracie through the doors. I had everything crossed. If I'd made a mistake, this would be yet another setback.

Like hundreds of brides before her, Gracie stepped up. I could hear her breathing so held her hand. "Open your eyes."

There were gasps all round. Gracie stared at the mirror. Gradually, a smile grew. "Oh, my God. I have a waist. Look, Huw." She swung herself around from side to side. "I have a shape. I have arms."

"You're amazing, cariad," Huw said. "Just beautiful."

Gracie turned trying to see the back. Claire brought a mirror. "It fits at the back." She smoothed down the dress and caught her finger.

"Bloody hell. It even has pockets—a wedding dress with pockets."

I wiped away a tear. These moments meant everything.

"I don't care what it costs, this is my dress." She stared at me. "You are a miracle worker. In some shops, they didn't even let me try anything on, in others they told me they could alter things, but they didn't look right. This dress could have been made for me. It's perfect."

"It is perfect," Ingrid agreed. She stepped forward, and hugged Gracie. I had the feeling a friendship was being formed before my eyes. Both she and my mum were brushing away tears.

"I wish you could be there on the day to help me dress," Grace said. "I'd pay. It's in September. I suppose Oswestry is too far."

"I don't know," I said. "Claire might be able to go." We'd helped before if we were near enough, but Oswestry might be a challenge. "Now we'd better get you out of the dress and box up all you need. We have shoes you might like too."

"I need a wide size nine," she said.

"We have shoes to size eleven and always wide."

We waved them off an hour later. Claire made coffee and we sat.

"I can see now why you love this job," my mother said.

"We were lucky today."

"It's not luck," Claire said. "Chrissy has such an eye. She listens to what women want, and she knows our stock. I'm learning so much working with her. I can't tell you what a joy it is to come to work every day. Sometimes, it takes more than one dress, but we haven't had a failure yet."

Ingrid wrapped an arm around me. "Every time you do that, more people will learn what you do. I'm so proud to be your sister-in-law."

I leaned into her. "I'm glad to have you too—all of you." I heard a low mooing sound nearby. "Would you like to see the Highland cows? They have the cutest babies, and it sounds as if they've wandered nearby. They're often in the field behind us."

Once outside, we strolled along the path at the side of the glamping pods to the field. The cattle stood in a group munching on fodder. Across the field, Rob and my dad waved. In the distance, Amy stood whistling. Suddenly, the Blacknoses appeared through the gate followed by Ralph.

"Oh, it's those cute curly ones," Mum said. "And they have babies. Do they milk those?"

"No, they're for the tourists," I replied. Amy waved.

"The dogs are so clever," Ingrid said.

"Amy is Beth's daughter. She and Ralph have won prizes at sheepdog trials." I noticed Dad and Rob making their way back to us. Amy walked behind them with Ralph at her heels.

"I'll leave you to it if that's all right. I've revision to do for my A-levels. It's been fun showing you around."

"The fun's been ours," Rob said. "Dad got to drive a tractor with Jed supervising. Thank you."

"I did. It was massive."

We waved goodbye to Amy. I wondered how Beth was getting on with her meeting. "So what are you lot doing this afternoon?" I asked.

"Lunch somewhere, then we're off to the little railway line.

Your dad can sit. We'll visit a few villages, take lots of pictures, then be back for dinner at the hotel tonight. You will be joining us, won't you?"

"Of course," I said. "George is a great chef, and it's quiz night." I already knew Beth would be there. Now, all I needed to do was not touch her too much, or gaze at her like an adoring puppy. I could do that, couldn't I?

# 17. Beth

I missed the quiz. Instead, I spent the evening with my head over the toilet bowl throwing up. Clearly, I hadn't warmed those leftovers thoroughly enough. The next day was much the same. By Friday teatime, I was able to eat toast smeared with Marmite without rushing to the sink. Throughout the last two days, Amy had kept me supplied with drinks, and I had texted Chrissy with apologies and questions, and told her to stay away in case I had a case of winter vomiting virus.

Still tired, Friday night I took to my bed early and caught up with more of a crime series I'd started watching. My phone beeped and I paused the screen—a text from Chrissy.

*How are you now?*

I pressed out a reply. *Much better. Stopped spewing and ate some food. Sorry I missed seeing your parents again.* I took a sip of peppermint tea and waited for her reply. To be honest, part of me was glad not to have faced scrutiny from anyone. I wasn't ready to talk to Karen. Like Jed, she was good at getting the truth out of me.

*They all had a good time. Mum and Dad are back home now, and Rob and Ingrid are in Edinburgh for the week. Rob asked some pointed questions but I neither agreed nor denied. I don't like lying to him. They had a great day out in Whitby on Thursday. Mum said she could see why I like the place, and they might book a glamping pod in the summer.*

"You all right, Mum?" Amy put her head around the door. "I've done all the chores. I'll be in my room if you need me. Uncle Ned's back, on crutches, giving orders to the dogs and sheep. Seems he insisted on coming home from his daughter's."

I chuckled. "I bet Daisy is thrilled to have him return. And thanks for everything over the last couple of days. Hopefully, it'll be business as usual tomorrow. I'm sorry about missing the trials."

"It's fine. Zoe from school is showing her dog as well. She has her own car, so I'm planning to stay with her, and she lives nearer to the venue than us. You're sure you are okay to be left?"

"I'll be fine. The worst has passed now." I had plans to spend more time with a certain someone. Talking of which, my phone beeped again. "Got to get this," I said. "It's Karen."

Amy grinned stepped back, then closed the door behind her.

*Sorry. Amy popped in to check on me. She's away tomorrow night so I was wondering if you'd like to have dinner with me. I hope I'll be OK by then.*

Fingers crossed.

*I'd love to have dinner. Claire and I will be busy all day, but she's got a date with this new bloke so wants to leave early and is getting a taxi home. Have you thought any more about wearing some dresses for me. I have the perfect one which is different to the norm I'd like to photograph you wearing. I do love to play dress-up! Come over here about five.*

Saturday would be a busy day for me too. All of the pods were booked and needed cleaning. I usually helped to speed things along. Nonetheless, curious about what Chrissy had in mind, I wrote:

*I'll see you at five. xx*

The thumbs- up sign I received made me smile. I settled back down with my computer.

By mid-afternoon, the figures and words were swimming in front of my eyes. Everything had stopped making sense. I'd had a quick sandwich at lunch and put a casserole in the slow cooker. I was ready for dinner later. I decided to treat myself to a couple of hours streaming a film. I couldn't remember the last time I'd watched a whole one at home. I grabbed a coffee and settled onto the sofa.

My phone woke me minutes after five.

"Sorry," I said, when I saw Chrissy's name come up. "I fell asleep watching something. I'll be over in two shakes of a lamb's tail."

"No hurry," she replied. "Claire has just left."

I ran upstairs and checked my face and hair. I added make-up for the photographs and piled my hair into a ragged bun with strands falling everywhere. I decided against changing clothes, although I did have on one of my few matching bra and panties sets. If I was going to spend the next couple of hours in and out of dresses, I wanted my underwear to be less on the practical and accommodating side. *You really do want to please her if you're prepared to do this.*

Ten minutes later, I strolled into the shop trying to act as if I was more confident than I felt.

"I'm back here with the dresses," Chrissy called. "Come through."

Chrissy was stood staring at one of the racks. "I'm picking out different frocks to the ones Ingrid and Claire have modelled for me. You've got more of an hour-glass figure than they have —they're both more pear-shaped. I think the corseted ones will suit you better and you have the upper body to fill them."

I glanced at my chest hidden under my usual dungarees and jumper. I'd become used to hiding my curves because they were wider at all points than fashion deemed suitable. "Thank you," I said, attempting to accept the compliment. "I wasn't sure what to wear underneath. Should I have worn shapewear to smooth everything?"

Chrissy stepped into my personal space. "You're beautiful as you are. I love how you've done your hair. Now, you're sure you don't mind indulging me. I can't afford professional models yet."

I took a slight step backwards to calm my racing pulse. "No. It's only trying on a few dresses, and I've worn one before, but not as beautiful as these. Are these the other photographs?"

Chrissy picked them up. "They've come out well, haven't they? Rob is going to add them to the website, and I'm getting poster-sized versions to display on the walls here." She turned to the dresses. "Now, let's start with this one."

The first dress was a simple satin dress with tiny straps, a nipped-in waist, and an A-line skirt. It had built in cups. I turned away, removed my bra, and stepped into the dress. Chrissy pulled it up, then used the ribbons of the corset to tighten the back until it fitted perfectly.

"These shoes should suit you."

I stood in the heels which, thankfully, weren't too high,

while Chrissy placed a veil on my head. She walked me to the podium, and I stared at myself in the mirror. I hadn't looked this beautiful on my own wedding day, even though I'd been several stones lighter.

Chrissy stood behind me, gazing over my shoulder into the mirror. "Gorgeous. Plain suits you. Maybe I could add a few flowers in places or a belt. I've set up a green screen for you to stand in front of to take the photos. Rob can add whatever background then."

I stood in the poses Chrissy suggested with a bouquet of silk flowers just like a bride would on her big day. We repeated the process with two other dresses, both more elaborate and more expensive. Each time, Chrissy stood behind me, staring into the mirror, telling me how beautiful I looked, touching me to make sure the dresses fitted perfectly. Her breath ghosted over my bare shoulders, and I longed to have her kiss me, to watch her kiss along the naked flesh while I stared into the mirror.

"Now," she said, taking my hand and leading me back to the dressing area. "I have something different for you to try. It's a full outfit with lingerie to match." She reached into a drawer.

"The corset has hooks at the front making it easier to do up. It'll barely cover your nipples—the dress will do the rest. There's knickers and stockings which attach to the corset. I can help or leave you to it and come back to fit the dress."

"No," I said, taking a deep breath. I attempted to smile and laugh. "It's not like you haven't seen me before, or hundreds of others, I assume." Truth was, I wanted to show off. Wearing those other dresses had made me feel beautiful but also sexy. I wanted to be sexy for Chrissy. I liked that she wanted to look at me, and I wanted to please her. I stood, naked underneath the robe she'd given me.

"Okay then." She handed me the knickers first. They weren't quite thongs but were probably the smallest pair I'd ever worn. I stepped into them, and they skimmed my stomach when I pulled them up. Chrissy took out the corset and held it up. I had to admit the colour was beautiful—midnight blue. The fabric shimmered. It was designed to sit over a person's hips providing a way to push out a dress, accentuating the waist. Suspenders hung from the bottom edge in four places.

"Okay, as I said, this has hooks at the front but has ties at the back which can pull you in at the waist. Are you ready?"

I nodded and let the robe slip from my shoulders. Chrissy gave a small but satisfying gasp as I struggled not to cover my breasts. Despite their fullness and the fact that forty was my next birthday, my nipples still pointed straight ahead. I'd always worn good bras since my corporate lawyer days. I pulled my shoulders back and lifted my arms. Chrissy placed the corset on my body from behind.

"If you can do a few hooks, I can make sure it's in the right place."

I began to do them up with shaking fingers while Chrissy shifted it until it sat right. I turned and she did the rest. I almost did fall out of the top. The stockings completed the look, showing a stretch of white thigh. Chrissy turned me around again.

"Imagine being a bride on your wedding night and peeling your dress off to reveal this ensemble underneath." I stared into the mirror feeling astonished it was me staring back. Chrissy loosened my hair from the headband, and it fell around my shoulders.

"Now, for the dress. I've always hoped someone would choose this someday. It reminds me of those dresses grand ladies wore to balls in the past. It's a real princess dress. You'll need to step into it, and I'll pull it up. It has tiny dark pearl buttons up the back."

The skirt was huge and covered with tuille, which shimmered with thousands of tiny stars like the night sky. The silk bodice covered enough of me to be decent. I slipped my arms into the ruched sleeves capping my shoulders. Chrissy placed a necklace around my neck—a beautiful sapphire and silver pendant.

"It was my great-grandmother's," she said.

Finally, she attached a veil to my hair then handed me a pair of shoes I wasn't sure I could even walk in. "Time to go out there," she said leading me through to the show room. "Close your eyes."

My spine tingled. I imagined being blindfolded and only feeling while Chrissy walked behind me. My feet touched the podium and I stepped onto it.

"Open your eyes and see how magnificent you are."

I did. I blinked a few times. The skirt spread around me. The corset and dress pulled in my waist. My pale creamy bosom —which I'd always hidden, now appeared just right. I could have stepped into *Bridgerton* and danced the night away—well, except for the veil.

"I look..."

"Stunning," Chrissy supplied. "Simply stunning. Keep your head held high. I need to take some pictures."

When she'd finished, Chrissy stood behind me. She removed the veil, pushed my hair to one side and kissed the back of my neck. I shivered. She continued the kisses along my shoulder to the top of my arm. My breath hitched and she wrapped one arm around me and slipped it inside the bodice of the dress. One finger reached my nipple and pressed.

"Yes," I gasped. "Oh yes." I knew I was already damp in anticipation of more touches.

She pinched the nipple between two fingers—hard enough to cause a little pain.

"Please," I said, not knowing who the hell was saying these words. "Please, harder. Make me feel." My body ached. When she stopped I wanted to shout out, to protest at the loss of her touch. Behind me though, she undid the dress and guided it to pool my feet. Now, I stood on the podium in front of three mirrors wearing only the underwear, and I didn't care.

Chrissy kissed my neck again. This time she bit where neck met shoulder then licked the same area. She slipped her arms around me and undid a few of the hooks. She crossed them, taking a breast in each hand and squeezed each nipple again. I leant my head back and closed my eyes.

"No, I want you to see. I want you to see me touching you."

I opened my eyes. She lifted my breasts above the corset, exposing them. "Oh, God."

"You, Beth Nethering, are the sexiest woman I've ever met. I wish I could bend you over and fuck you right here while you watch."

Without thinking, I wriggled out of the knickers, stepped from the podium, and stood with my legs apart. Chrissy gathered the dress out of the way.

"I wish I had my strap-on here. Maybe next time." She reached over and grabbed a chair then put it in front of me. I bent over letting my breasts spill forward. She reached between my legs to push her fingers inside me, not the easiest of angles, or most elegant of manoeuvres.

"You're soaking," she said.

"Are you surprised?" I pushed back, fucking myself on her fingers. "So good."

Somehow, she managed to reach one finger forward to my clit and rubbed while clasping my breast with her other hand and holding me close We moved together, me in the lingerie, and her in her suit, still fully dressed, which added another level of something to the whole event.

"So good," I said. "Please don't stop. Oh yes, there, please. That's it. Don't stop. Make me come. Please. I need to come."

I squeezed, knowing I was probably hurting her hand, but I didn't care. I didn't care about anything else in the moment. Deep inside me, the feeling began. Like something ready to burst, it grew and grew. Everything tightened then exploded out of me. I struggled to catch my breath. I expected to see stars, and I did. I held onto the chair as my knees buckled, afraid of fainting, and Chrissy held onto me, and didn't stop touching me until I could take no more. Then, I was empty again and back down to earth. I opened my eyes to see a woman I hardly recognised staring back at me. I had no idea what to do with the image or the woman.

"I need to pee," I said as panic rushed through me. "I need to..." I stepped out of the shoes and hurried back to the changing room. I struggled to get my breathing under control, and I wept. What the hell had I done? I'd let someone I barely knew finger-fuck me in front of a mirror—exposed myself, body, heart, and soul. I slipped my still stockinged feet into my boots and grabbed my coat, glad I'd brought the long one. I had to get out of there. I couldn't face Chrissy. I couldn't face anyone. I lifted the handle on the fire escape door and ran back to the house without glancing back. Once inside, I locked the door and fished my phone from the pocket.

*I'm sorry.* I texted with shaking fingers. *Please don't follow me. I need time. Tonight was too much.* I leaned against door wishing Ralph was there to cuddle as my knees collapsed from under me, and I ended up a weeping mess on the floor. What had I done? And where did I go from here?

# 18. Chrissy

I didn't sleep. I stopped trying around four in the morning and dragged myself out of bed to the kitchen where I sat watching birds flit across the courtyard, clutching a large mug of tea. I'd already been through what had happened over and over again, examining everything, worrying if I'd put any pressure on Beth. Had I missed some sort of consent, or was this simply a case of cold feet—of shock at discovering something about herself Beth couldn't deal with? Question after question spiralled through my mind so quickly, I couldn't pin most of them down. It struck me I needed someone to talk to, someone who might understand, but there was no one, not even a cat.

After the divorce, I lost my wife and my best friend. Judy had been my assistant in the shop. We'd known each other from school. I was the person who had introduced her to Molly. I'd shared all my doubts, suspicions, and concerns with her, not knowing she was the one sharing my wife's bed, or rather our bed. Then, at least, I had Rob to talk to, but I couldn't talk to him about this. I had no one, and I'd never felt so lonely in my life.

Tears dripped from my cheeks. I had a business. I had an employee. I had a contract to honour. Had I ruined everything? I liked Beth. I fancied Beth. Had I moved too quickly with someone discovering aspects of themselves? I'd been there myself. I remembered the shock of realising I was different to my friends—how I'd gone online to see what those feelings meant. My first fumbles with another girl had frightened the life out of me. But I'd been lucky. My parents had supported me, and my twin had been my rock. Did Beth have someone to talk to? I glanced at the clock. Somehow, a few hours had passed. I needed to get ready for work. We had an important customer today—a friend of Lady Phenella, who had specific ideas of what she wanted for her wedding dress, and money to spend. I took out my phone and typed a quick message to Beth.

*I'm here if you want to talk.*

I hesitated but then pressed send. If Beth needed space, I'd let her have it.

Claire practically skipped out of the back door of the inn then got into the car next to me. "Good night?" I asked, glad it gave us something to talk about.

"Wonderful. We went to this Italian place and talked and talked. Matt comes from a medical family. His parents are GPs. He's originally from the Welsh valleys. He has this lovely sing-song accent. We're going to Whitby tomorrow."

"He sounds promising. I'm glad." At least someone was happy. I glanced in the rear-view mirror to see an impatient idiot driving far too close to me.

"Stupid bastard," I said as he pulled back in when a car appeared once more. I stopped in the next lay-by, not prepared to risk my life for his stupidity and thumped the steering wheel.

"Are you all right?" Claire asked. "You've dark circles."

"I didn't sleep much last night—I sometimes get insomnia And that reckless lunatic doesn't help." I checked the mirror and set off again. .

"Mum gets that. When she does, she bakes, and we wake up to the smell of cookies."

"Baking isn't my strong point," I said.

"It's awful when you can't sleep. I used to be terrible as a child. Mum says I never wanted to miss anything."

My heart dropped when I saw the sign. I always looked forward to work, but not today. We were likely to have an awkward client, and being knackered often made me fractious. I hoped coffee would help. Thankfully, no one had arrived before us.

"Did you get those photographs taken with Beth yesterday?" Claire asked as we exited the car.

"Yes, we got some, but then she had farm chores to do. I'll show you, then we can decide on which pictures to get in poster-sized copies. We have a good variety of dresses."

Once inside, I left Claire organising the show room and headed for the kitchen to make coffee. I opened the changing area to discover Beth's clothes still there. Shit! Had she run out wearing just the underwear and her coat last night? The heels were still there along with her dungarees, jumper, briefs, and bra. I gathered and folded them, then hid them in a wedding dress cover. I glanced through the window in the direction of the house, wondering how she was this morning. I made coffee and took one to Claire.

"Lady Mallory wants a strapless dress with a fishtail, so we'd better get a few out. She's a size twenty-two. She's bringing as veil as well that's been in the family for years."

"Fishtails don't suit everyone," Claire said, practicing her diplomatic tone.

"They don't, but we should let the bride decide. I think she's bringing her mother and her four bridesmaids. It might be useful to make sure we have drinks available even this early. And I think I hear a car or two pulling in."

Lady Mallory entered followed by five others. "Hi," she said offering her hand. "I'm Mallory, and this is my mother and my four best friends in the world."

I shook the proffered hand. She had a firm grip. "I'm Chrissy, and this is Claire. Would everyone like to sit down?" All of them gathered on our padded bench seating.

"It's a surprise to find a place like this here in the middle of nowhere. I have to admit my daughter has driven us mad trying to find a dress. I said we could have one made. You are our last resort."

"People think we have money to burn," Mallory said. "All I want is a decent dress at a decent price. Too much money is being spent on this wedding already." She glanced pointedly at her mother. "*Some* people have to be reminded who is actually getting married." Mallory turned to me. "My fiancé is a climate scientist who abhors waste. This is why I'm using the family veil."

"Could I see?" I had a few ideas spinning in my head.

Mallory pulled a box out of a large bag then opened it. The lace was old and exquisitely made. "It's Honiton," she said. "With a leaf pattern."

"It's beautiful. I can understand you wanting to use it. We've picked a few for you to try and, I may have a wildcard choice. Why don't you come through?"

Mallory rejected four dresses outright. The first she tried on was satin, pulled in at all the right points with ruching around the bust and hips, and a layered tulle fishtail. One glance in the mirror followed by a glance at her entourage gave me the answer. Next, she chose a busier dress with lace and sparkle, but the top wasn't right. Two more dresses were tried on and rejected.

"About this wildcard you suggested."

"How do you feel about previously worn dresses?" I asked. "I have something I bought at a house clearance sale a few years ago. I know you didn't want anything specially made, but I might be able to adapt it. The lace is similar to your veil with a similar leaf pattern. Come through to the back and see what you think."

Mallory sighed. "I'm open to anything at this stage, otherwise I'll be heading down the aisle naked as the day I was born."

I'd had this dress in storage with others I'd collected over the years. As a student, I'd toured shops and attended auctions. I checked the rail and pulled it out. "Now, you wanted something strapless and with a fishtail."

"I have curves I'm not afraid of showing off, and smooth shoulders."

"Good for you," Claire said.

Mallory disrobed again without concern. Claire and I lifted the dress over her head. "As you can see, it has a sweetheart line which covers your bust. Originally, the dress had some shoulder covering, but everything was detachable then to mix and match. It's corseted but the boning is made from spiralled steel. The dress is over a hundred years old from before World War I."

"Really? And the steel is comfortable?"

"As it can be. It might be worth practising for the big day.

The corset is long and goes over the hips. I can keep the dress narrow by making clever alterations. As for the fishtail, this one has layers of net covered by the lace and a decent-sized long train. I can change it to whatever you like." I placed clips down the back to pull it in and added the all-important veil.

"Okay, let's see." She stepped forward carefully. I made a mental note to check on walking needs.

"Eyes closed everyone," I instructed. With assistance, she stood on the podium facing the mirrors.

"Okay, open your eyes."

Gasps came from everyone.

"It's beautiful," Mallory's mother said. "Is it Honiton lace too. That dress could have been made with the veil."

I stood back. "It'll need taking in, but we've plenty of time for changes," I explained. "But I can guarantee that no one else this season will have a similar dress."

"It's vintage, Mum. It's gorgeous. I love it." She turned and hugged me. "Thank you so much. What do you think, girls?"

Her bridesmaids crowded around, and tears flowed. I high-fived Claire. "Now, we'd better get you out of your dress and pack it away safely. I'll need to take accurate measurements, and absolutely no dieting for the big day—not with a dress like this."

"I wasn't planning to," Mallory said. "What you see is what you get, and Steffan knows that."

At midday, I sent Claire off then sat in my office. Beth hadn't replied to my text. I glanced through the photographs I'd taken. She was so beautiful in the blue dress. I knew I wouldn't sell it. This was Beth's dress now. Why did I do this to myself? Why could I never take care with my heart? I'd always tended to fall quick and fall hard then declare my feelings too soon.

Well, not this time. This time I'd wait for Beth to come to me, and if she didn't, I'd have to deal. She had more to worry about than me. Everyone knew I liked women. I couldn't imagine what it must be like for Beth to get to nearly forty and discover she could behave so wantonly with another woman. I closed my eyes and saw us in the mirror, heard us breathe, smelt her perfume, felt the warmth of her skin under my fingers, and remembered the taste on those fingers after...

*Stop it.* I shifted in my seat, conscious of the damp between my legs. I wept bitter tears. I wanted to feel her in my arms, to sit on the sofa with her and watch telly, to see her face when she showed me around the farm—so proud—to comfort her when her grief welled up, and to laugh with her as she chased the chickens and ducks back into their night-time accommodation. I wanted to stand behind her with my chin on her shoulder and my hands in the front pockets of her dungarees. But for now, all I could do was wait. For now, everything was out of my hands and in hers.

# 19. Beth

I sat slumped in front of my computer screen the Wednesday after that night. I'd read the same detail several times and still nothing was getting through. This sort of contract was bed and butter to me—literally. I provided legal advice for many of the farmers in the area on commercial law as another income stream. But today, the words swirled and nothing stuck. Instead, my mind kept taking me back to Friday night with Chrissy, to what I'd done with Chrissy. And how much I'd wanted to do it.

I'd been wanton. There was no other word for it. I'd wanted to wear those clothes. I'd wanted her hands on my skin. I'd wanted to see her. I'd wanted every second of the pleasure she'd given me—pleasure unlike I'd ever experienced—meant solely for me. Everything Chrissy had done had been for me. She'd asked for nothing in return. From that night, my every spare thought had been about touching her. My concentration was shot. I'd been over and over what I'd allowed to happen so much it scared the living daylights out of me. Every night since I'd pleasured myself thinking about her—not only the sheer joy, but the comfort of having her arms around me in bed. I don't think I'd realised how lonely I was, or how starved of touch I felt.

A knock on my office door bought me swiftly out of my musings. Jed put his head around the door.

"Jed. I wasn't expecting you. Is everything all right?" All I needed now was bad news.

"Two things."

I swallowed hard. "Okay. What's going on?"

Jed sat. "Tony Shaw turned up this morning. He wanted to see you, but I managed to persuade him I'm in charge of purchasing."

"That doesn't surprise me. What did he want?" Tony Shaw had been my brother's friend. They'd hung about together from primary school. I'd never understood why. He'd bullied Neil and made fun of him. It was as if he had some hold over him. The man was also a misogynistic bastard who thought women shouldn't be allowed to run anything, let alone a farm, and he'd never held back from telling me so.

"He wanted to sell us a new tractor, or anything really. He offered to provide our feed for less than we pay. He was most insistent. Reading between the lines, I think his business is in trouble, which wouldn't surprise me. He drinks most of the profits. He left shouting the odds—how we should consider ourselves less than men working for a woman. He was lucky not to get Dad wrapping a crutch round his head."

"But he's gone," I said.

"And told not to return."

"And the other thing?"

"I had a call from Sam over at Daleside. They've had one sheep killed and another two injured—a dog they think.

169

They're letting all the local farms know. It could be tourists with a pet let off the lead who haven't said anything. They've had trouble with gates being left open and sheep straying."

This happened every so often. "I'll give him a call. None of our visitors have a dog with them, but we have thousands of tourists, and no matter how much publicity there is about keeping dogs on leads, many don't believe *their* precious pooches will worry sheep. Hopefully, it'll be a one-off. The last thing we need is a sheep worrier on the loose. It wouldn't be the first time someone has dumped an unwanted animal in the countryside. I assume the police are checking into it."

"Apparently. I could put more cameras up," Jed said.

"Good idea." I closed my laptop knowing I wouldn't get back to it today. "Anything else I should know about?"

"Not that I can think of. Everything's running smoothly. Milk production is good. The lambs are growing. Have you heard anything about planning permission for more pods?"

"Not yet, but you know those wheels grind slowly. How's Ned? Did he escape your mum's clutches again this morning?"

"He did. He's grumpy and driving Mum to distraction. He complains about every programme on the telly and sneaks out like today if Mum doesn't keep an eye on him. He's got a check-up next week. And what about you?"

"What about me?" I didn't meet his gaze. I didn't dare. He'd see right through me.

"Oh, nothing really. I met Amy clearing out Geoffrey this morning. She said you'd been tetchy over the last few days."

"'Tetchy'?"

"Well, distracted then. If there's something you want to talk about with an adult not your daughter, then I'm always available. Why don't you come over to ours tonight? Lars is cooking." Lars was almost as good a chef as his brother.

"I don't think so. I've this contract to check for John Holding. Every penny helps." I didn't want any difficult questions with a possible audience.

"You look tired."

I sighed. "I've had a touch of insomnia. I'll get over it. Now, is there anything else?" I'd not meant to be dismissive.

Jed frowned and stood. "No. Though..." He stared straight at me. "Maybe I'll pay a visit to Chrissy and see how she's doing."

"No, please Jed, don't. I'm asking you as a friend not to."

"So there is something going on, and it's serious."

"I can't tell you—not yet. My head is all over the place. I'm not ready to talk to anyone."

"Not even Chrissy?"

"Especially not Chrissy. I just can't. I made a big decision coming back here. I've worked hard getting this place in profit, taking enough to live on, and ploughing everything in to keeping the family legacy alive. I've not allowed myself to think of anything other than Amy and this place."

"I know." Jed pulled his chair in closer. "Isn't it time you thought about yourself then? Amy will be at university next year. You're forty—"

"Thirty-nine."

Jed glared at me. "Okay, you're forty soon, and you deserve a life too. You deserve some fun."

I'd had too much so-called fun—so much I'd scared myself. "It's complicated," I replied, lacking other words.

"Is it really? Or is that an excuse not to take a risk?"

I buried my face in my hands. "I don't know. Facts and figures are easier to deal with than feelings."

Jed lifted my chin so I faced him. "Yes, but they don't keep you warm at night, cause your senses to tingle, or make a mug of tea when you need one. You've let yourself be alone for too long."

"Maybe that's it. Maybe I'm to set in my ways. Look at me. I spend my days dressed in dungarees and wellies. I'm fat, and I found a grey hair last week."

Jed took hold of my wrists. "Stop it. You are beautiful. Clearly, Chrissy thinks so. I watched her when you did karaoke. She didn't take her eyes off you for a second. Anyway, some of us prefer partners with a bit of flesh on their bones. When Lars wraps me in his arms, I know I'm safe. Okay, the fact I know he can swing an axe like a Viking helps, but when he takes control, takes..." Jed stared, a slight smile crossed his lips.

"All right. I hear you." I knew Chrissy liked how I looked. That much had been crystal clear from the beginning, but I hadn't been such a woman before, one with no inhibitions, and it had scared me, shattered my comfort zone and how I'd come to see myself.

Jed's phone beeped. He checked it. "It's Joe. He's seen a dog near the old bothy running around on its own. I'd better get out there."

"Keep me informed," I said. "I'll ring Sam now. If you can catch it, please try. We've no idea where it's from. It could have been dumped and be scared."

"I'll call the vet. We'll do our best. And think about what I've said."

I kissed his cheek. "Thank you. I'm lucky to have you as a friend."

"You are." He stood and grinned at me before heading out through the door, phone already next to his ear. I reached for my phone and called Sam's number.

I didn't return to work but instead decided to throw myself into creating a cottage pie for dinner.

"Mum." I turned to see Amy stood in the doorway, taken by surprise because usually the door would slam, and she'd have shouted from the hallway.

"Hello, love. Cottage pie for dinner in about an hour. I'll see to the chickens and ducks first. Good day."

"Yeah. Fine. I'll see to Geoffrey." She turned and exited without saying anything further, leaving me wondering what was going on. Amy always informed me about her day over a drink at the table before seeing to her horse. I heard about lessons, her friends, her teachers, what she thought about anything that had happened during the day. I cherished those conversations, knowing a lot of parents had children who communicated through grunts, but Amy and I were close. Something was up.

I put the mince and veg in the casserole and topped it with swede and carrot mash with an added sprinkle of cheese then slid it into the oven. I knew from experience Amy would come to me with whatever was bothering her.

There was still a nip in the air at night if the day was sunny. I grabbed my coat and herded the birds back into their overnight accommodation. Occasionally, especially when they had young, foxes attempted to get into the coops, so we'd built them stronger. I picked up a couple of stray eggs from birds who'd laid wherever they were stood then shooed them in. Across the way, beyond the bushes which separated farmyard from the bridal barn, voices drifted through the silence, along with the odd mooing noise from the cows. My breathing increased and my heart pounded. What if she was coming here? I tried to move, but found my feet were frozen to the spot. The sound of a car engine and wheels over gravel told me Chrissy and Claire had departed. I leaned over with my hands on my knees attempting to take air into my lungs, then once I'd let the fear pass, hurried back to the house.

Amy was sitting at the kitchen table when I got back. I joined her and waited.

"Mum."

"Yes, love."

"You know we usually talk about anything."

My mind leapt in every direction attempting to pre-empt anything Amy might want to talk about. We both took a breath, and I reached out a hand to cover hers.

"Yes, love. Is there something you want to say?"

She gazed at me. "It's nothing to worry about. I'm not pregnant or anything." One crossed off the list.

"It's just..." I tightened my grip. "Well, for us it's not a biggie, but it might be for you. I don't think it will be with you having friends like Jed, and Chrissy is gay as well, but you see the thing is, Mum, I think I might be bisexual."

"Oh." My brain attempted to find the right words. "You think? Do you have feelings for someone?"

"I do, and we've... You know I've had sex before."

Heat rushed into my face along with memories of recent events. I needed to push those thoughts away and concentrate on my daughter.

"Am I being embarrassing. Mum? I can shut up. I wanted to bring her to meet you. We met at the trials last year. She comes from a farming area too, a few miles over the border into

Cumbria. She's a first year at university on the same course I want to do. Her family have a sheep farm. She was really interested in our milking sheep. Said she'd tell her father."

My brain uttered the words, *young people today*. "I'd love to meet her," I said. "Are you two... going out together?" I wasn't even sure what label such relationships were given now. *Shit, I feel old.*

"We've talked about it. I like her, Mum. She's such fun, and she loves farming. She rides. We have a lot in common. You know how a lot of the people in my school want to go to university to get away from here."

*Like I did.*

"But Tash and I want to learn to help us be better at farming."

"And is Tash bisexual too?"

"She describes herself as pansexual if she has to—her full name is Natasha. She's not into labels. She says she loves who she loves. I mean, why stop yourself experiencing all the possibilities?"

*Why indeed?*

"So, it's okay if I invite Tash here for the weekend sometime soon? She wants to see the farm and meet you."

"Of course it is, darling."

The timer let us know dinner was ready.

"And..." She hesitated glancing at me through her fringe. "I want Tash to sleep with me. You're not going to be funny about that, are you?"

I sighed. "No, love. I'm not going to be funny. You'll be eighteen soon."

"And you'll be forty even sooner."

"Thanks for the reminder. Now, I'd better get dinner out

before it burns. There's a bottle of red on the counter breathing. Could you pour a glass? And yes, you can have one if you want."

"Nah, I'll stick to fizzy water. They all taste like vinegar to me." She stood. "We're all right, aren't we, Mum?"

I moved and wrapped my arms around her to pull her into a hug. "Of course we're all right."

I glanced at the door. Chrissy would be in her house now probably sitting down to a ready meal with her feet up and a glass of wine. Maybe she'd had a great day. Maybe she would be thinking about me—about us. I pulled away yet still held my precious daughter with my hands on her shoulders.

"I love you whatever. All I want is for you to be happy and to live your best life." Perhaps it wasn't too late for me to make a few changes in mine too.

# 20. Chrissy

I stared at my emails. Among the usual bookings and enquiries was an invitation to a surprise fortieth birthday party for Beth at the White Hart, organised by Karen Petterson with apologies it was last-minute. I had no idea how to respond. If I didn't accept, Karen would want to know why. If I accepted, it meant I had to face Beth. I wanted to see her more than anything, but I had no idea if she wanted to see me. So many times over the last few days I'd begun to write emails or texts, or I'd picked up the phone to call. Not once had I pressed send.

Claire entered the room behind me and placed a coffee on the table. "Did you get the invite from Mum? Beth said she was ignoring getting to forty, but it's difficult to stop Mum when she's gets the bit between her teeth. Organising a birthday party in three days is nothing to her. You will be coming, won't you? I want you to meet Matt properly."

I hesitated. "The accessories supplier is coming on Saturday afternoon, but I should be able to be there. The posters of you and the others wearing the dresses have arrived as well."

"I can't wait to see the backgrounds your brother added," Claire said.

I hadn't dared open them to see the ones of Beth. Claire passed over the large tubes. "Can I see?"

"Help yourself."

She peeled back the tape and removed the plastic top. "I've dressed the mannequins in the new designs by the way. The plain satin one is beautiful, and I love the cloak with the fur trimming for winter weddings."

"We always have to cater ahead," I said.

Claire pulled out the posters and attempted to flatten them. "Oh my God. These are amazing."

"Considering I did them."

"True," Claire replied absentmindedly. "But you've an eye for what works." She lay them on the table. "I've never seen myself like this before."

"You suit everyone one of those dresses," I agreed.

There were nine posters, three of each person in three different dresses ready for display. I'd already bought the frames. Claire continued to look through them until she got to the one of Beth wearing the midnight blue dress.

"Wow. Is this really my Aunty Beth? I'm so used to seeing her in jumpers and dungarees, I forget she has a great figure, and with her hair down... If she ever gets married again, she needs to wear that dress."

I had no words. Beth was spectacular, and I knew the smile on her face was for me. I'd caught her just right. I didn't want to share her with anyone else. Instead, I wanted to hide the poster away and keep it for myself.

"I'm telling you, everyone will want a blue dress when they see this. She's like something out of *Bridgerton* or *The Gilded*

*Age*—like a princess ready to go to a posh ball." The shop bell rang. We had no one booked in until later but people did sometimes simply turn up. We both hurried next door to find two people glancing around the room.

"Hello, "I said, stepping into our main display room with Claire following. "Can we help you?"

"We saw the LGBTQA+ flag on your website." I noticed the sculpted eyebrows of the other person and wondered.

"We're getting married in the summer."

"Congratulations."

The speaker glanced at the other man for support. He smiled encouragingly. "You see, what it is, well, I'm a drag queen. We met at a club. Nigel knows who I am and loves me anyway. He wants me to be married the same way I see myself, not in a straitjacket of a suit. I'm John, by the way. In my other life. I'm Fiddle-Dee-Dee. I do stand-up, cabaret, and I'm a torch singer. So, I need a wedding dress. There will be other queens at the ceremony, so it needs to be the most flamboyant and over-the-top dress ever. I want all eyes on Dee-Dee as she walks down the aisle. He thread his hand through his partner's arm and gazed at me. "Can you help?"

"We'll do our best. And I can embellish any dress however you want. So, what do you have in mind?"

"Big. I want big. I want a dress like they wear in Victorian times that's so wide it'll sweep up the aisle hitting anyone either side. I want the narrowest waist I can get into. As a queen, I have quite a chest—hence the double D. I want lace and sparkle. I want a dramatic veil Nigel can lift from my face. I don't want burlesque. I want princess with a capital *P*. I'm not a small person, so when I saw your website and the company name... I want everyone to get the same message—this is me. I want to shout from the rafters this is who I am, and this wonderful man wants to marry me. So, I thought I'd see what you could offer."

No one could say I didn't love a challenge. "Just give me a few minutes," I said. "Claire, could you get my laptop? Would you like something to drink?" It was tea all round.

"Please take a seat." I sat between them and opened the laptop when Claire returned.

"When I was a student, I created dresses for a bunch of drag queens, including a wedding dress." I found the film of the evening. The final dress on the catwalk had the shape John wanted with a skirt covered in ruffles.

"Maybe," John said. "It's a starting point."

I spent the next four hours helping Dee-Dee to find the perfect dress. Nigel was sent away. I pointed him in the direction of the village. Creating a dress was similar to solving a jigsaw puzzle, taking bits from others until we made a whole.

"I need to do my face. I need to see the full effect." Claire and I sat fascinated as John became his alter ego. It was like watching an artist create a pictures as each piece of make-up was applied using different products, strokes, and colours to shape and decorate. Finally, Dee-Dee pulled a wig from the box. It was big and blonde and reminded me of a certain country singer.

"There," Dee-Dee said. "This is me."

Claire and I set about layering the outfit from underwear to veil until we'd pinned or tacked everything together.

"Close your eyes," I said, and we led her to the show area and the mirrors. Dee-Dee stood on the podium, eyes still shut with the dress and train spread around her. "You can open your eyes now."

"I'm scared to."

Claire and I each took a hand. "You can do this."

For a moment, Dee-Dee stood and starred. She wasn't a parody. She was a bride. Different from others perhaps, but still a bride.

"Oh. My. God. I can't believe it. I look…"

"Simply stunning."

"I can't cry. I'll ruin the make-up." She turned from side to side swishing the dress. "This is one huge fuck-you in a dress. Fuck you to everyone who ever called me names and tried to make me feel bad about myself. I am John, but I'm also Dee-Dee. This will be our day. Somehow, I found this wonderful man who is prepared to put up with me and loves me. He is the kindest man I've ever met. And the sexiest." The last part was whispered.

Now, all three of us were crying. I handed out the tissues. "Claire and I will put it all together for you then call you in for fittings."

"Whatever it costs," Dee-Dee said. "This is a present from my grandmother. She died a few months back and left me the money. She always encouraged me to be whoever I wanted to be. She was a scientist. I never knew exactly what she did. It was all a bit hush-hush. I used to wonder if she was a spy. I loved her so much. Anyway, this is for her too."

We packed everything away carefully. There were several hours of work left yet to complete the look.

At the outer door, John took hold of my hand. "Thank you. I shall be singing your praises to everyone so you may get a few calls."

"It's been our pleasure," I said.

Nigel waited with a huge smile. John hurried towards him, gave us a wave, and climbed into the car. I turned to Claire.

"That's what I call a good outcome," I said.

We walked back into the shop, tidied up then sat in the office drinking cappuccinos from the new machine.

"You *will* be coming on Saturday, won't you?" Claire said.

"Yes, I'll be there. And Matt be joining you?"

Claire blushed. "He will."

"And everything is going well with you two?"

"It is. Excellently. We've..." I guessed where this conversation was heading.

"And?"

She sighed. "All I can say, is everyone should be so lucky."

"I'm happy for you—truly. Now, let's have lunch then I need to sort through the paperwork. Sadly, these accounts won't do themselves. You can secure the posters and refresh the accessories selection on display before the salesperson is due. We'll get away a bit early today."

Later that evening, unable to settle to anything, I knocked on the house two doors down. News travelled fast along the row of houses, and I knew Mrs Flood had fallen a couple of days ago, leaving her unable to take her dogs for a walk. I pushed at the door, and it opened.

"Hi, Mrs Flood. It's Chrissy from a couple of doors down."

"Oh, come in, love. It's good to see someone."

I found her sat in her armchair with the dogs now alert to the new person in the house. Both wagged their tails. "I need a walk," I said. "I thought the dogs might need a run out too. And if there's anything else you need."

"Bless you, love. My niece will be around soon. She likes to feel useful. But I suspect these two would love a walk. What about it, lads? Would you like to go walkies with the nice lady?" The cockerpoos jumped up immediately, wagging the whole of their rear ends with excitement.

"Their harnesses are in the kitchen."

I got them ready. "I won't be long," I said.

"Sometimes a good walk helps you think. And I too love a good natter. You know what they say—a problem shared is a problem halved. Though I don't believe that—really."

"Thanks." I had no idea how she would deal with lesbian love trauma. "I'd better get these two out."

Dotty and Lucy pulled me along happily as they sniffed every piece of grass and hedge alongside the river. The area had been landscaped, providing paths and stopping places with benches. The evening was warm and the air full of the fragrance of blossom beginning to appear on trees. I said hello to a few others with dogs and pulled the girls away. The river wasn't wide at this point and trickled over rocks creating, along with the bird song, a pleasant background noise. At the half-way point, near an old packhorse bridge, I stopped and sat on the bench. Dotty and Lucy, being well-used to their owner's stops, settled on the bench either side of me. I took a couple of treats from my pockets and fed them. I needed to decide how I would play meeting Beth again at the party. I could simply go, stay on the down-low, and wait for her, or I could dress myself to the nines and show her what she was missing. Maybe, I could do both—set out my stall and see if she wanted to buy.

Why did everything have to be so complicated?

"It's all right for you two." Then again, I'd seen the pair snuggled together in one bed, and I was sure the other would pine if one was to shuffle over the rainbow. My phone vibrated in my pocket. I took it out—Rob. There was that twin telepathy at work again.

"Hi," I said. "This is a nice surprise. Everything all right with you?"

"I have news." The excitement bubbled in his voice. "You're going to be an aunty."

"Wow, that's brilliant. I'm so happy for you both. When's it due?"

"Middle of October. I can't wait. Mum and Dad are thrilled. What about you? How are things?" He paused. "And how is Beth?"

"Beth is complicated."

"Ah."

"Ah, indeed. We haven't spoken since last Friday. Beth did some modelling for me, and one thing led to another. I think she scared herself, Rob. I think she's discovered things about herself, and she found it hard to cope. I know I should feel guilty turning her life upside-down, but I don't. I like her. I like her a lot. She's good company in all sorts of ways."

"But this wasn't the first time you'd been together."

"No, it wasn't, and I'm not going to explain what made it different to my brother. Let's say, I think the sex in her marriage didn't bring out the best in her."

"What are you going to do?"

I nodded to someone passing by and held onto the girls when his dog showed interest and barked.

"Where are you?" Rob asked.

"I'm sat on a bench alongside the river with two cockerpoos who belong to one of my neighbours. She's hurt her ankle so I'm walking them."

"Getting to know the locals already, then?"

"A few. As to what I'm going to do—it's Beth's birthday on Saturday and they're throwing a surprise party for her. No-one has realised anything, so I've an invite. I thought I might wear something sexy and see what happens. I don't want to pressurise her..."

"But you want her to know what she's missing as well. Sounds like a plan. Keep a clear head. If she doesn't want you, as Dad would say, you put it down to experience."

"Thank you for those wise words. And now these two are getting restless again. I'll see how it goes."

"She'd be lucky to have you, sis. Don't forget that and take care of yourself."

"Don't worry. I will. Give my love to Ingrid. Maybe I'll start knitting something." I finished the call and stood, shaking my legs back to life. "Come on then, you two. I have an outfit to plan. Faint heart never won fair lady."

# 21. Chrissy

It had been an age since I'd dressed to impress. I took out my black velvet skirt and waistcoat from the wardrobe. I'd already chosen black underwear, making the most of my bust, and black lace-patterned hold-up stockings. I pulled on the skirt, which hugged my hips then checked on the ribbons at the back of the waistcoat that had been specially created for me. It had black leather and velvet panels and hooked together at the front. It could pull my waist in by four inches if I wanted, but such torture took practice. I settled on being able to breathe, but even this setting helped to give me hips. Silver chains hung attached from the sides to the tiny pockets as if each had a watch attached to the end. I wore nothing but my bra underneath, giving me a cleavage. Finally, I took a shoe box out and carried it downstairs. There was no way these babies were going on my feet until all I had to do was walk from the car to the building. These were taxi shoes not meant for anything practical. Like the rest of the outfit, they were leather and velvet. Many might consider a slim four-inch heel not too difficult to walk in, but I spent my life in sensible flats. These shoes hugged my feet. They weren't strappy or flimsy, just beautifully made for me by a friend at university.

I glanced in the hall mirror. I'd thought about blood-red lipstick but instead had settled on something less obvious. My hair hung loose and framed my face. I was dressed for a party, and whatever happened, I intended to keep my head, not drink too much, but also set out my stall for the woman whose birthday we were there to celebrate. Okay, I wasn't being subtle, but...

I grasped my jacket and put it on, then grabbed my keys and the shoe box. Outside, the evening was still warm and dry—perfect for a party. I parked my car at the back, slipped my spare glittery and foldable slippers into my bag, and stepped into my heels. I wobbled a little, took some steps and got into the swing. The back entrance to the inn took a visitor along a few corridors past the kitchen and the toilets then into the main bar. I'd been told the birthday girl would arrive at eight. I intended to find a corner and stay there. Noise echoed from beyond the next door. I removed my jacket and slung it over my shoulder then made my entrance. The room was busy, and I felt many pairs of eyes staring at me. Jed stepped forward out of the group to greet me.

"Fucking hell. Can you even breathe?" His gaze surveyed me from head to toe.

"I can," I said. "It gives me a figure."

Lars joined us. "It certainly sends a message."

I stared at him. "You know."

Jed scowled at his husband. "Lars, get us a drink, please." He turned back to me. "Let's sit down. We need to talk."

I nodded and followed him. "I think maybe we do."

From the corner, I could see Karen glancing in my direction. Lars placed drinks in front of us then wandered off, leaving us alone in the corner. I swallowed several mouthfuls of the white wine I hadn't asked for.

"Okay, so you're here. What's going on between you and Beth?"

I stuck out my chin. "I could answer that it's none of your business." I hoped I sounded more confident than I felt. I had no idea how much Jed knew.

He sighed. "Sorry. Let me start again. I know you and Beth slept together because she told me. She needed someone to talk to—"

"And she figured you'd provide the gay angle, huh?"

He shrugged. "Maybe. But she needed to talk to someone. She's not had feelings for another woman before—sexual or otherwise. It's like everything she ever thought about herself has come crashing down around her. And she's been through so much. As a teenager, she had her life mapped out—get off the farm, become a great lawyer, get married to a great bloke, develop her career, have a couple of kids. She couldn't understand why I wanted to follow in my father's footsteps when there was so much of the world to see. And now, she's back on the farm, divorced, and finding her sexuality isn't what she thought it was, along with hitting forty today."

"Well, they say life begins at forty, don't they?" My attempt at humour fell on deaf ears.

"Just tell me. Are you serious about her? I know you've recently been through a divorce and a major change of life yourself. Are you willing to help Beth negotiate her way through more change? It's hard enough to be a female farmer. She's faced misogyny and patronising attitudes from others, not to mention all the speculation about her brother's death. This relationship will become common knowledge. Small places—people gossip. And they know you're gay."

I gulped more wine. "I've never made a secret of it."

"No. Me neither. Attitudes in farming are slow to change, but they are changing. I've had the odd comment over the years, and I bet some women wouldn't choose to come to your shop because they'd think you were ogling them."

"That's nonsense," I protested.

"Of course it is. So, are you in this for the long term?"

"For fuck's sake. I don't know. I thought my marriage was forever, but here I am. Do I fancy Beth? Oh, yes. Do I have feelings for Beth? I think so. But it's been weeks not months. She'll get to make the decisions. You do realise that, don't you? I've given her space. I want more, but if she decides to pull away, I'll live with it."

"You won't fight for her."

"That's unfair. I'd fight if I thought there was a chance. But I'd respect her choices too." The lights flashed in the bar and silence settled over the area.

"Beth is here," Karen whispered. "Quiet everyone."

We waited until the door from the car park opened. When it did, everyone shouted, "Happy birthday" then the singing broke out. I joined in with the rest. Beth stared around the room until her gaze found mine. I gulped. Heat burned in her eyes, and determination in her expression. She said something to Amy then headed straight for me.

"Am I all right to join you?" Beth said, sitting before I could answer.

"I'll get you a drink," Jed said. He kissed Beth's cheek. "Happy birthday."

"It's good to see you," I said. "Happy birthday." She was

wearing a figure-hugging midnight blue velvet dress that accentuated her every curve and created a magnificent cleavage. She wore her hair around her bare shoulders. Clearly, I wasn't the only one who'd come dressed to impress.

"Do you like the outfit? I choose it from a place in York. You said this colour suited me."

I sipped my drink. My mouth had suddenly become as arid as a desert, unlike other parts of me. I'd heard the feeling described as a groin twitch but seeing her I ached. I licked my lips. "It could have been made for you," I said.

"Good. I wanted to feel special. I spend so much time in dungarees and wellies."

"Well, they're practical," I said. "You can't wear a dress riding a quad bike." My corset seemed tighter, and I had to remember to breathe. Heat rose in my face, and the room seemed to have become so much warmer.

"I like your outfit too," Beth said. "And I don't think I've seen you with your hair down, even when we..."

Jed appeared with Lars and Karen. They sat and handed out gifts. Others in the room came to talk too. I sat back and sipped the rest of my drink.

"The function room is all ready for the buffet and dancing," Karen said. "George has set up a barbeque outside as well. You know how he loves to cook meat outdoors. We couldn't let your fortieth go by without a party." She stood and held out her hand. "There's karaoke as well and you're first up."

"Really?" Beth replied. "Shouldn't the birthday girl get a pass?"

"Nope, but I am singing with you."

Beth glanced at me. "Please tell me you're not planning for us to sing *It's Raining Men.*" Karen pulled Beth up, and those of us there for the party followed them to the large room at the back.

For the next thirty minutes, we had no chance to talk as the birthday girl was busy chatting to others in the room. I people-watched and nodded to those I knew. Lars joined me, carrying a plate of burgers and salad, which he placed on the table.

"Help yourself. My brother makes a mean burger, all from scratch." Around me, others were tucking into food, so, knowing there was no way to politely get my lips around it, I took a large bite.

"Wow," I said after I'd chewed the first chunk of beef. "That's something special." I took another bite.

"I know," Lars said. "He won't even tell me what's in the patty"

I demolished the first one in minutes and eyed eating a second but felt hands on my shoulders. The perfume told me it was Beth.

"I need to whisk you away," she whispered into my ear. "Follow me."

"Okay." I wasn't going to argue even to eat another of those fantastic burgers. She walked away. I stared at the back of her. The heels made her hips swing. It was mesmerising. Lars poked my arm. I stood and followed her out of the room and along a corridor. She opened a door and pulled me in. I glanced around.

"I can't remember the last time someone pulled me into a toilet," I said.

Beth turned me around, pinned me against the wall, then kissed me as if it would be the last time. She wrapped her arms around my back and held my arse. I was thoroughly and gloriously kissed, closed-mouthed then open-mouthed with tongues. She nipped at my lips with her teeth before I lifted my chin, and she kissed my neck then sucked on an earlobe. If I'd been wet before, I was soaking now.

"Fucking hell. Where did that come from?" I gasped.

"There are things I need to say. I need you to listen." Beth stood with her gaze fixed on me.

"I'm listening," I said.

She took a deep breath. "You touch me like nobody else has ever touched me. You see me like no one else has ever seen me. You've made me see a different part of myself, one I didn't know existed. That night, in those mirrors, I saw the desire in your eyes and in mine, and suddenly, I wanted to experience everything life and love had to offer. I let myself go in order to discover another me, a different me, not the one everyone sees. I felt... alive. The world was full of incredible sights and sounds. You gave me so much, but then I wanted to do the same for you. I wanted to touch you, to smell you, to taste you on my tongue. I wanted to bury my face between your thighs, and it scared the fuck out of me."

I wanted to say she didn't need to be afraid, but I stayed silent, attempting to keep my breathing and my body on an even keel.

"There I was, dressed in those sexy clothes wanting you to want me."

*I did. I do*

"I saw myself and I panicked. Embarrassment won, and I ran."

I reached and stroked her hair. "You didn't need to run. We could have talked."

"I wasn't ready then. I've always thought things out before. Maybe I've not always made the logical choice and gone with heart not head, but with you all decision went out of the window followed closely by rational thought. And now...and now my daughter has told me she's bisexual and has a girlfriend. I wanted to say, me too."

*Oh.*

Her hand brushed my leg. "This skirt is too bloody tight. I want to touch you." She pushed it higher until she reached bare flesh. "You're wearing stockings."

I moved my legs apart, and she moved her hands until... "Please," I whispered.

She explored with her fingers until they touched my clit. "You're so wet," she said, her lips millimetres from mine. "I want to make you come and kiss you at the same time."

I gasped again and pressed my mouth to hers. We both moaned. I was so ready for this. I writhed, trying to get her to the best position, all the while struggling to breathe through my nose and praying no-one walked past or wanted to use the room. I was so close. I hoped my legs would hold me. I closed my eyes letting a wave of sensation run though me, which culminated at the end of her fingers. I couldn't maintain the kiss any longer and threw my head back but held onto her.

"Yes," I said. "Oh, fucking yes." When I opened my eyes, she was staring at me with a satisfied smile.

"You are so beautiful," she said. She removed her hand, brought it to her face and sucked each finger clean. "You taste good too."

"I need to sit." I closed the toilet lid. "Are you all right?" I asked.

She knelt beside me. "I'm fine because tonight you're staying here with me. Karen thought I might be too drunk to go home and kept me a room. Jed says Amy can stay with him."

"But?"

"But nothing. I told Karen about us. She wasn't as surprised as I thought she'd be. I think Jed may have told Lars who told George who hinted to Karen. Welcome to village life. So we have a room, and the walls are thick in this old place. Will you stay?"

Who could resist such a plea? Not me, that was for sure. "I'd love to, but now I need to clean up, and despite having eaten one burger already, I'm starving. I also want to dance. This is a party after all—your party."

Beth struggled to her feet in her heels and washed her hands. "Don't be long."

"I won't," I assured her. She unlocked the door and opened it slightly.

"The coast is clear."

Left alone, I stared in the mirror. A lot of me couldn't believe what had just happened. I tidied myself, pulled down my skirt, then applied more lipstick. I couldn't help smiling.

*Time to party. The night is yet still young.*

# 22. Beth

I couldn't believe what I'd done. I'd pulled Chrissy into the disabled loo and touched her. I'd had sex in a toilet. Me. Boring old Beth Nethering had brought a woman off at my fortieth birthday party in an inn owned by my best friend. And this time I wasn't going to let my fears overwhelm me and run away. This time, I intended to eat, drink, dance, and be merry.

All my life I'd lived with one foot on the brake. Even when I'd made the big decisions, I'd weighed each option, balanced pros against cons. Yes, I'd sometimes gone with my heart or my gut. This time was for me. The farm was ticking over with all the usual problems. My intelligent and beautiful daughter was about to begin her own journey and would need me less. Why shouldn't I do something for me? Maybe I'd end up having an exciting affair. Maybe I'd find something and someone for life. Whatever. I'd reached forty and intended to take the bull by the horns, which seemed appropriate. I pushed the doors open to the function room and made my entrance.

Amy appeared. "There you are."

"Sorry. I got distracted chatting about ice cream." Yeah,

pathetic perhaps, but my fellow investors were here, so it made sense as an excuse for my disappearance.

"Of course you did. Make sure there's salted caramel flavour in your range. That's all I ask. Have you eaten anything yet?"

Her words unnerved me. Had she seen something? I needed to tell her sooner than later. "No, and I'm starving. Look, there's Chrissy." I beckoned her over as if I hadn't just spent an exciting, if too short time, with her.

"We're getting food. Care to join us?" I asked.

Chrissy grinned. "Yes, please. I've built up an appetite." I hoped Amy didn't spot the glance that passed between us.

We sat eating burgers with all the trimmings, taking care not to drop anything on our outfits. Jed and Lars joined us, along with Karen.

"My daughter is a huge fan of yours," Karen said to Chrissy. Claire was dancing with her boyfriend who'd just come off shift.

"Claire is an asset," Chrissy replied. "I'm lucky to have her. She combines empathy with a great understanding of selling, and she's a quick study. I swear she knows the stock better than I do. I've had nothing but praise from customers. That outfit looks lovely on her. Matt seems like a nice bloke."

I listened to the conversation with interest. Karen didn't take prisoners or beat around the bush with people, and I wanted her to like Chrissy.

"Matt is lovely. He's exactly what Claire needs. Between him and you, my daughter has grown in confidence, and I'll be forever grateful."

"And Claire isn't the only one dressed for the occasion," Jed said. "You and Chrissy beat everyone in the room hands down. Can you breathe in that waistcoat, Chrissy?"

"I can and eat as well. It will go tighter than this, but I'd need to practice. It gives me a waist and hips, and almost boobs, otherwise I'm as straight as a pencil. My friend makes them for men too if you ever fancied one."

I laughed and nudged Jed as he blushed. Lars coughed into his pint.

"Have I hit a nerve?" Chrissy asked, feigning innocence.

I stood and slipped off my shoes. "I think it's time to dance," I said taking Chrissy's hand. "Come on, show me your moves."

We spent the next hour on and off the dancefloor until the music stopped and the lights were switched on. From the side, a trolley was pushed through the doors bearing a large cake covered in candles. The music rang out and everyone sang *Happy Birthday*.

Karen stepped onto the stage. "Thank you to everyone who has been here tonight, though I guess free food may have encouraged several of you. Now, I'd like to invite our birthday girl, Beth, to blow out the candles. And yes, there are forty of them."

I managed in two attempts and made my wish. The cake had a picture of the farm, complete with sheep and cows. "I need a photo before it goes," I said. Amy took out her phone and snapped a few.

"Speech!"

"Speech!"

"I don't intend to say much. Thank you to everyone here for coming to share this evening with me. I see so many people who I've known my whole life, and some who are new. In small villages like Netherington, it's hard to keep secrets, but it's also good because there's always someone to call on if you need help.

When I came back home ten years ago, I had no idea how my ideas would work. Every single person in this room has helped me in some way. I'd also like to say thank you to my daughter, who is off to university in the autumn."

"I've got to get the grades yet, Mum."

"And I have no doubt you will. Anyway," I lifted a glass. "To old friends and new friends, and happy birthday to me. Life begins at forty."

By midnight, I was worse for wear, and drink. People had plied me with drinks though I hadn't drunk them all—they'd have had to carry me upstairs, and I still had other plans. Most of the guests had left. Jed and Lars had taken Amy with them, although she protested she didn't need babysitting.

"How come you get to stay?" she asked.

"It's part of my birthday present. And I get to have one of George's breakfasts tomorrow. You've had a few drinks, and I don't want you home alone."

Lars took her arm. "Come on. The cats will be thrilled to see you."

Jed stood close enough to whisper in my ear. "And you have a good night. I'd say don't do anything I wouldn't do, but that still gives you some scope."

I thumped his arm lightly. "Go home and take care of my daughter." Earlier I'd given Chrissy the room key, and she'd left the party already.

Karen wandered towards me. "I think we'll leave this until the morning. Time for bed."

"Thank you," I said. "For organising this and for..."

She stopped me. "We both know life can be short. Fuck what anyone else thinks and live every day. This is my new motto. My kids are grown-up and happy. The business has survived the last few years. I'm forty as well. Time to live a little before we begin to wonder what the point of all this graft was. After all, no one's dying thought is likely to be I wish I'd worked longer hours, is it? I might even give George a good time before I tell him I've booked us a two-week holiday in Canada next year so I can go whale watching like I've always wanted."

I hugged her. "You go, girl. George is a lucky man."

"And Chrissy is a lucky woman."

I leaned back so I could see her face. "We're both lucky."

Ten minutes later, I stood outside the door. I lifted my hand to knock but stopped. Instead, I pushed the door open. Chrissy lay under the duvet. Her bare shoulders and neatly piled clothes revealed she was almost certainly naked. I shut the door and locked it.

My pulse quickened. I wasn't sure if it was fear or excitement "I need a few minutes in the bathroom."

"You wouldn't be intending to get undressed and into one of those fluffy bathrobes without me seeing now would you?"

Heat rushed into my face. "Um, this dress required stronger undergarments, and there's nothing sexy about shapewear."

Chrissy sat up and folded her arms across her chest on top of her knees. "I disagree. I love the slow reveal of flesh as you lower the fabric."

I laughed. "You are a weird woman. Anyway, I need to use the loo and clean my teeth. Meaty, oniony breath is not anyone's idea of a good time."

"I'll be waiting for you."

"I'll hurry." And I did. I emerged wearing the robe and nothing else. Chrissy had dimmed the lights, but it wasn't dark.

She pulled back the duvet. "Please come join me."

I slipped the robe off and jumped into bed. Despite my

resolution not to care, being in bed with someone still made me uneasy. Chrissy moved my arm and positioned herself next to me. She flicked out her tongue at my nipple, then took it in her mouth and sucked hard.

"Oh," I squealed. "Sorry, you took me by surprise."

She reached over and tweaked the other one, making me wriggle even more. For a full ten minutes, my breasts got more attention lavished on them than they'd had in years. I writhed with pleasure, arching my back to make her take more. Her tongue swirled and her fingers pressed and pinched until I couldn't take such a sensation overload. As if reading my mind, she stopped. I stared into her eyes which were now mostly black with what I hoped was desire.

"I bought something to use," I said, blushing furiously. "I wasn't sure. I researched online, but now I only want you to bury your face between my legs."

"We can do whatever you want," Chrissy said. She gazed at me turning her head to one side. "But I'd love to know what you bought. You can always tell me when I'm not gazing at you, and if I have my face in your pussy, I'll definitely be otherwise occupied."

She pressed kisses down my body and settled with her cheek resting on my thigh. She twirled a couple of strands of longer hair—I trimmed but didn't shave.

"I'm glad you're more au-naturelle," she said.

I tried to relax.

*You're a forty-year-old woman who's been married and had a child. You shouldn't find the fact someone has their face so near to your pussy so unnerving.* Heat had rushed into there and into my face.

"So what did you buy?" Chrissy asked. She used her fingers to open me up and slipped one then another inside me.

"I." My voice squeaked. "I got this vibrator which has two ends so it can go into both of us. Oh God. So good."

"Toys are fun," Chrissy replied. "But I prefer being hands-on, and fingers in, and tongue pressing." She shifted position but left her fingers inside me. Her tongue hit my clit and I lurched.

"Sorry but fuck me, that feels good."

Chrissy lifted her head. "I'm fucking you." She added a third finger, making me feel so full. The sounds she made. I panicked about how wet I must be, but Chrissy pressed harder or sucked on my clit. I lifted my pelvis, wanting more while my world centred itself between my thighs. Something bubbled deep inside me demanding to be let out. I attempted to slow things down. I didn't want this to end, but my body had other ideas. My orgasm built and built until it burst out of me. I grabbed the sheets and my muscles contracted around Chrissy's fingers.

Words babbled out of me. "Oh, God. Fucking hell. Don't stop. Yes. Oh, yes." Then I could stand no more.

"Please, "I said touching her hair. "I can't."

Chrissy lifted her head. Her face glistened in the lamplight. She licked me once more—a final parting.

"Wow," I said, trying to restore my equilibrium. "My orgasm--it came from so deep inside me like a huge wave."

Chrissy withdrew her fingers slowly and licked them clean. "I love the way you taste. Salty with the merest hint of onion. Mmm."

My face pinked immediately. I yawned.

"Sounds like someone is tired."

I was. I couldn't deny it. "It must be my vast age," I said. "I need to go to the loo as well—another sign of age."

I moved until I sat on the edge of the bed, stood, then hurried to the en-suite.

"Great arse," Chrissy called after me.

In the bathroom, I peed and dried myself. I gave my teeth a quick clean. The face in the mirror hadn't changed, but everything else had. This wasn't just a mid-life crisis. The more time I spent with Chrissy, the more I liked her and wanted her.

Back in the bedroom, I found her lying on her side facing me. I scooted round the bed and got in behind her. It felt good to have someone in my arms.

"Sleep now," she said. "I intend to eat the biggest breakfast ever tomorrow, and you can tell me about all the places you intend to take me to in this beautiful home county of yours."

I started making a list, yawned again, and the world drifted away.

# 23. Chrissy

"I can't remember the last time I came here." Beth said. "And look, they stock our cheeses. It's always exciting to see them out in the wild, so to speak."

I placed several truckles in different flavours along with biscuits for cheese in a basket. "I'll stock up."

"You don't need to pay. I can always get samples."

"No. I want to pay." I strode to the counter. "These, thank you. I've heard this variety is excellent."

The woman serving glared down her long nose then smiled. "Oh, they are. I love the one with apricot, and I wish they made the Christmas pudding variety all year round. They're all tasty with fruit cake and we serve them in the café upstairs." I couldn't resist, and beckoned Beth over.

"Beth here is one of the farmers whose sheep are used to produce the milk."

Beth blushed. "There are a few of us."

"But it was your idea," I said. "And you're introducing ice cream this summer."

"We are. We'll be launching the flavours at the Yorkshire

Show, which is now only a month away. There's so much to do. Anyway, come on. We've a lot to pack into today. I haven't visited the castle here either because Amy went with school. We can do more shopping after and buy something for lunch as the weather's been kind."

"It's funny, isn't it?" I said as we strolled through the market stalls lining the road. "I haven't been to many touristy places in Kent. In school, we used to go into London. I haven't even been to Canterbury Cathedral or any of the castles. We did go to Hastings once. I enjoyed our visit to the coast, though the rain stopped us seeing Scarborough at its best. I want to visit York Minster next."

"I've shopped in York loads of times," Beth agreed. "But I've not been to the museums or even to Jorvik, despite Lars working there. I did History A-level but liked the modern stuff more. So coming here to Skipton is widening my knowledge too. Amy loves the castle and the abbey. She loves the earlier times from her History A-level course." She paused. "Talking of exams, Amy is home tonight as she doesn't have a competition this weekend. And now she's had her last exam, I thought it might be ,time to tell her about us. I'd like you to be there."

I stopped, causing a man to bump into me. I muttered a quick sorry and hurried across the road after seeing a gap in the traffic. Beth followed me into the castle grounds. I paid the entrance fee and sat on the nearest bench.

"Sorry. I didn't think the street was the place for this conversation."

Beth sat next to me. "I did rather spring it on you. I don't like lying to her or at least being evasive. She's not stupid. She'll work it out. And she was brave enough to tell me. This seems like the perfect opportunity, and I'd like you to be there."

"Are you sure this isn't something for a mother and daughter chat? She might feel intimidated with both of us."

Beth chuckled. "My daughter doesn't do intimidated. I brought her up to state her views, and she's bisexual herself."

I wanted to be as confident. "But you're her mother. I mean, I think she should know, but I'm not sure me being there will be helpful."

Beth stared out over the green to the castle entrance. "I thought you might want to support me. I thought we could have dinner together, a few drinks, and you could stay over. But if you don't want to..."

*Shit! I've made a pig's ear of this.* I took Beth's hand, not caring if anyone was watching. "I'm sorry. You caught me off guard. If you want me there, I will be. This is new for me. Breaking news to parents is one thing, teenage children is another. Children don't like to think of their parents being sexual."

"Believe me. Parents aren't overkeen about their children and that aspect of their lives either. And remember, Amy has recently gained a baby brother. If her dad is allowed to have sex, then I am too, with whoever I choose."

I nodded. "Okay. You're right. I will be there. I want to get to know her better, anyway. Now, let's visit this castle."

We wandered around the place, reading snippets from the booklet about who had lived there and when. Both of us decided against going into the dungeon. Of course, we both had to see the toilet off the kitchen which was off the large banqueting hall. Beth gazed into the long drop over the river.

"Careful," I said. "It warns how people have lost their glasses and those sunglasses look expensive."

"I bet your arse got chilly sitting on the hole. I can't imagine what it must have been like."

"Crowded and smelly. Most people bedded down in the hall as it was nearest to the fire." We ambled back into the central court and sat beneath the tree. "It's still impressive though," I said. "So many are ruins. You can feel how people lived here, and that servants would be running around. The uneven steps are clever to catch attackers, and the stairs built the wrong way so you couldn't fight with a sword in your right hand. I feel the need to watch something with sword fighting. It's been years since I've seen *The Princess Bride*."

"Never seen it," Beth said casually.

I turned to stare at her. "Sorry. Did I hear you correctly? You've never seen *The Princess Bride*? Inconceivable! Well, that needs to be rectified, and tonight. Takeaway, confessions, wine, and a great film."

"Okay. But first we buy picnic stuff and spend an afternoon in a beautiful place. Lots of fresh air and incredible surroundings."

Bolton Abbey turned out to be exactly as Beth described. We stood at the top entrance to the valley and Beth pointed out the details—the church, the ruined abbey, and the grounds.

"Beyond the trees, are steps over the river. It's usually quieter over the other side. I've packed a blanket. Come on."

We trod the path carefully to the bottom. The abbey was a ruin but still gave an idea of how huge and isolated it must have been. "Those walls are so high. It's amazing how they built these places, getting the stone here so people could pray."

"The steps are over there."

I followed Beth but we found the steps were closed. I

breathed a sigh of relief as there were sixty of them. "We'll have to take the bridge."

We settled our blanket under a tree for shade and ate the food in the warm open air. From where we sat, we could see people making their way into the valley.

"It's beautiful here," I said, spreading pate on a chunk of bread. "And lovely to get away from work for a day, although Claire is helping at a wedding. To make up for it we've a few appointments tomorrow."

"It's nearly as demanding as farming," Beth said. "At least Ned is back now, and I can leave Jed in charge of everything."

"I was watching him with the sheep the other day. It's amazing how they follow him to the milking parlour. He hardly needs to use the dogs, and they know what they're doing without being told. I suppose they get used to doing the same thing every day. And don't they say sheep can recognise faces?"

"They do. They associate milking with food. Any time I do this sort of thing, I feel like I'm truanting, though I did feed the chickens and ducks this morning. Jed wants us to research alpacas or even llamas, but I'm not sure. I think we need to invest in more accommodation first. I saw this mad treehouse online we could build or something using railway carriages— anything quirky gets tourists interested."

"I guess diversification is the key to survival."

"It certainly is. There aren't many independent farmers now with each person having their herd of cattle or flock of sheep. Now there's so much paperwork, ticking boxes for everything from grants to tests. We're lucky I can do the legal stuff and Graham does the accounting. Most farms are in debt, especially if you need to invest in something new. It's all about long-term planning like you having the converted barn. You don't have to deal with steep high street rates, and I get a regular income. From the traffic I see, you're doing all right."

"We are. We've had visitors from as far away as Scotland and Norfolk. Online feedback has been brilliant. Rob's set up Instagram and TikTok accounts for us too. I leave that to Claire. I'm more Facebook."

I lay back on the blanket and stared at the sky, which except for a few scattered cirrus clouds, was clear and blue. I stared at the vapour trail of a plane flying overhead. "I always wonder where they're heading for and who is on the plane."

"I've not travelled by plane," Beth said.

I sat up on my elbows. "What, never?"

"Nope. We used to take the ferry or Eurostar to France for holidays when I was married, and now farming means I have so little time to be away. In fact, I can't remember the last time except for visiting Mum, and she lives in the north of France. Amy takes holidays with her dad, so I've never needed to. She's been to lots more places than me. What about you?"

"We used to go to holiday camps when I was little, but I've been to America, as well as the usual holidays to Spain and Greece. Maybe we could find time in the future."

"I'd like that."

"Me too." I turned to face Beth. "So we're agreed this is going somewhere then? Not that I'm putting any pressure on you at all." I wanted to give Beth time. Being in a relationship with her wouldn't change my life in the same way. My parents would worry like they always did, and Rob would do his impersonation of a big brother.

Beth took my hand and stroked inside my wrist. The lightest of touches sent my senses reeling. I wanted to pull her into my arms and kiss her.

"Tease," I said.

"More of an offer of what is to come." We gazed at each other and dissolved into laughter. "But first I have to tell Amy."

We spent the rest of the afternoon talking, planning where we might go, what we might do, acts and theatre shows we'd like to see, discussing our childhoods, our friends, past experiences, all the while stealing little touches here and there. I couldn't bear to be so close and not be in contact with some part of her body. I loved making her laugh with stories, and she told me all about growing up on a farm, though she didn't say much about her brother. Eventually, it was time to go.

We didn't talk much driving back to the farm. We sang along to the music on the radio, but I think Beth was absorbed in thinking of how she would speak to Amy. I decided not to disturb her thoughts. Luckily, the traffic decided to be kind and we made good time. Ralph greeted us at the door and sniffed at the boxes of takeaway we'd picked up.

"We're back," Beth called out. "And we have pizza." Sounds of the TV came from the living room.

"Let's take it through. I'll grab plates and drinks. Fizzy water okay? I think I was to keep a clear head."

"Water is fine. Give me the boxes." We found Amy sprawled on one of the sofas watching something on her laptop. She stopped it when we came in and glanced up.

"Good day?"

"Lovely," I said placing the pizza on the coffee table. Beth joined me on the other sofa. "We went to Skipton Castle and Bolton Abbey. Such beautiful countryside."

"Good. Mum needs to get away from here every now and again. Jed said to tell you the second milking is all done. I've checked on the Valois, the Herdwicks, and the coos, and given

Geoffrey a run out this afternoon. The new visitors have all arrived with no problems. All I need to do is sort out the chickens and ducks."

"Thank you," Beth said. "I can deal with the birds later. How was Ned?"

"Same as always. He says several walls need fixing, and the bothy in the third field needs repairs to the roof. He'll take the bike out again tomorrow and check everything else. I think he's glad to get away from Aunty Daisy." Amy filled her plate with garlic bread, pizza, and coleslaw.

I sat up. "Amy, I've discovered your mother hasn't seen *The Princess Bride*—which I consider to be a crime—I intend to rectify the situation tonight. We're going to stream it now if it's okay with you."

Amy laughed. "Mum is useless at films unless they're court dramas. I'll watch it again. As you wish."

We both laughed and Beth glanced at us, confused.

"Just eat and watch the film," I said, settling in.

Amy and I chuckled throughout and spoke the famous lines along with the actors. Every so often, Beth's fingers touched mine. From fizzy water, we moved on to fizzy wine. I couldn't remember the last time I'd been so happy and content until the film ended and I recalled Beth's intention.

Amy stood. "I think I'll go upstairs now and leave you both to it."

Beth straightened up. "Umm, Amy. Could you give us a minute? I've something I need to tell you."

Amy sat on the arm of the sofa. "It's fine, Mum."

"Sorry?" Beth said and glanced at me.

"You and Chrissy—it's not an issue. Well, I'd be a hypocrite if I had problems with you two, wouldn't I, considering? Did you think I wouldn't notice the looks passing between you and the little touches here and there, not to mention the amount of time you spend together, including the night of your birthday. I have to tell you you'd make lousy secret agents. I'm glad, Mum. In this life you go for whatever and whoever makes you happy. And I'm happy you won't be alone when I go off to university."

"So, you're fine with me and Chrissy?"

"May I remind you I have a girlfriend. I'm about to go upstairs, put my sound deadening headphones on, and talk to her online. Please don't worry about any noise."

I snickered into my hand. The wine might have had some effect. Beth's mouth fell open. I nudged her chin back up with one finger. "I think your mum is a little shocked," I said. "And thank you."

Amy stood again. "You're welcome. And don't worry. Everyone else will be fine too."

"I'm not sure about your grandmother," Beth said, finding her voice again.

"Nan will cope. She has her own life and a boyfriend. And that's what it's all about, Mum—being happy. There's too much misery in this world to let the chance go by."

Beth stood and wrapped her arms around her daughter. "How did my little girl get to be so wise?"

"Sensible parents, and a decent education. Now, I'm going up. Ralph." Ralph rose from the floor and wagged his tail. "Come on, boy." She disappeared through the door and Beth plonked herself next to me. I grasped a glass.

"Well, here's to sensible daughters." I swallowed a mouthful and kissed her. I intended to spend the night kissing Beth a lot more.

# 24. Beth

*A month later*

We started loading before six in the morning, knowing these would be three long days, but the Yorkshire Show was part of every farmer's life in the area. As well as the animals, we had a food stall for the cheese, and an ice cream stall for all the new flavours. If it was anything like last year, the place would be full-on all three days, and this year the weather gods were smiling after last year's downpours.

"That's Bonnie and Belle sorted," Jed said, and I ticked off my list. The mother and baby Highland cow category was one we had high hopes of winning with. We were also entering three breeds of sheep—the milkers, the Valois, and the Herdwicks—adults and lambs. Ned was entering his prize vegetables. and Daisy her dahlias, and Amy was participating in the agility contest with Ralph. Even this early in the day, the heat was oppressive. I wiped my brow.

A car pulled into the yard and Chrissy stepped out wearing

boots and a T-shirt advertising the wedding shop. I was still getting used to her having short hair, but the cut suited her face. The shop was closed for the day so Claire could also attend the show. Such occasions allowed for a lot of networking as well as groaning about farming.

"Room for me?" Chrissy asked grinning.

"You know there is." I kissed her cheek, not caring who saw. "I hope you're ready for this. We need to get to the showground early as traffic builds up quickly."

"Rob and Ingrid will meet us there. We'll sort out a definite meeting spot. At least the organisers provide maps of the different venues, and lots of places to sit. Ingrid is finding pregnancy tiring but she wanted to come."

"Are we done?" I asked Jed.

"Nearly, just the Herdwicks to load then we can set off in convoy. I'm driving the sheep in the big van, and Joe is hauling the cows. You can get there in your own car with Beth and Amy. Thankfully, we don't have to deal with the produce."

"No, though I'll have to help on both stalls over the three days. Right then, time to set off and eat big breakfasts once we arrive." I turned to Chrissy. "It's daft. The place is full of food stalls, but we rarely get time to eat. You ready?"

"I am."

"Come on, you two stop gabbing," Amy yelled from the car. Ralph barked his impatience to be off and running too.

The journey took less than an hour, but the traffic was heavy. This was the biggest show in the local farming calendar with both livestock and machinery as well as stalls selling everything from a potted plant to a huge combine harvester. Some reviews complained it had become more about the sales than the display.

"Rob and Ingrid are on their way," Chrissy said.

"I won't be able to spend much time with you today, I'm sorry. I'll make it up to you another time."

"I'm sure you will," Chrissy replied.

Heat rushed into my face. I wasn't used to flirting with my girlfriend, especially in front of my daughter. The news of our relationship had rushed through the local area like wildfire. The first quiz night at the inn had been excruciating with all the nudges and whispers. In the end, I'd made a bold decision and at next karaoke night, in the middle of singing a duet with Chrissy, I'd taken Chrissy's face in my hands and kissed her then finished the song and explained.

"Yes, the whispers are true. Any questions, keep them to yourself, and any problems, likewise." I'd grabbed a shellshocked Chrissy's hand and walked off the small stage to our seats where Jed and Lars failed to not shake with laughter. We'd joined in until tears ran down all our faces.

Once on the showground, we found where our animals would be stalled until the time for their classes. Unloading went smoothly, and I chatted to other farmers about the usual subjects—the weather, feed prices, stock prices, milk quotas—farmers always had something to moan about. Jed, Ned, and the other lads sorted the sheep and cattle and were in charge of making sure each animal was shown at their best. They chatted to the stewards who would be taking care of the animals for the next few days and making sure each turned up at the right competition.

Chrissy nudged me. "Rob messaged me to say they're by the fruit and veg tent. I'm going to go find them. I've noted the times of the various classes, so I'll try and find you, and I'll be back for you and Ralph, Amy." She wandered off with her phone in hand.

"I need to get to the cheese stall then the ice cream van," I said to Jed. "I'm sorry to love you and leave you."

"We've everything in hand, Boss. Livestock is our job, and shmoozing is yours. Got your talk ready?"

"Yep." I patted my bag.

I checked in at the cheese stall first, where every flavour and type we produced from the softest to the hardest variety was on display and available for sale. Jacob, one of the other farmers in their group was already there.

"Everything looks great," I said.

I was in my element here, explaining all about the products and tastes

"Hello, everyone. My name is Beth Nethering and this is Jacob Ross. We're part of a group of Dales farmers who milk our sheep. We make yoghurt and cheese, and our latest venture is ice cream." A few people from over the border into Cumbria and Lancashire expressed an interest in learning more, and I invited them to the farm and to see how the business worked.

Finally, ready for a drink, I turned around and found myself face-to-face with my brother's self-called best friend, Tony Shaw. I couldn't stand the man, and hadn't seen him since the funeral, always leaving Jed to deal with him if he turned up at the farm. I'd never understood why Neil had hung around with him.

"Neil would hate all this," he announced without preamble. "He was a proper farmer—old school. Raise your animals and sell them. He'd be turning in his grave if he had one."

My hands formed into fists. Fuck, I wanted to hit this man

so hard. I'd wanted to do the same when he'd spoken at the service.

"I bet your father wouldn't like it either, but then he's dead as well. And now I hear you're a lesbian. I'm not sure what's worse, milking sheep or being a pervert."

I clenched my teeth, and tried to tell myself the views of this man had no effect on me. I noted he appeared older than his fifty-five years. He'd lost his hair and developed bags under his eyes. "I won't say it's good to see you, Tony because it seldom is. I for one, have not missed your presence over the last ten years. And I don't know about you, but I've work to do. We're launching a new line of ice creams here today made from sheep's milk. You do know sheep are milked all over the world, don't you?"

"Foreigners. What do they know about farming? All I'm saying is Neil wouldn't like it."

"Maybe not, but the farm is doing well. Diversification is the key to survival these days. My family have farmed this land for hundreds of years, and I intend to make sure they keep doing so. Yours used to as well until your father cut his losses and ran. How's the feed and machinery business doing? We're using a new strategy in our pastures this year which will hopefully save us having to buy more food in. *Not that I'd ever buy from you.* There's lots of new ideas out there, Tony, and you've got to move with the times in farming."

He scowled.

"Oh, and I was sorry to hear about your divorce. I liked Janice. I hear she remarried and moved south. And you're a grandfather now, I believe. Though I expect you don't get to see the grandchildren much with them being in New Zealand.

Well, I must be going—busy day and everything. I'm checking out a new glamping pod design. We're expanding. People love to come here to holiday, but they expect the best and that's what Nethering Farm gives them. Have a good day."

I turned and yes, I flounced out of there. I didn't look back. By the time I reached our ice cream van, I'd managed to calm down. I was pleased to see a queue had formed. The van was the simple old-fashioned type. We'd even set up a Mr Whippy style vanilla flavour with a flake and all the sauces. We'd decided on eight flavours to start off with. I waved to Merry, another of our group. She'd inherited her farm around the same time as me and we'd met at the presentation on producing sheep's milk.

I opened the back of the van. Merry turned and smiled. "We haven't stopped," she said. "You'll be busy later. Lots of people asking about sheep's milk products for their kids. I think we've handed out as many leaflets and brochures as we have ice creams."

"Well done. We need the supermarket contract."

"We could always try pitching on *Dragon's Den*. It's worked for others."

"Maybe." I checked my watch. "I've got to go. We have an entrant in the Highland cow mother and baby class." I messaged Chrissy to let her know where I'd be and made my way over to the parade ring in time to see Jed leading out Bonnie and Belle. He'd done a great job with both of them. I sat on a bale of hay and watched. The judges examined mother and calf, who behaved impeccably. I had high hopes of a rosette for these two but there were other pairs equally as cute. I watched the others until a familiar voice spoke behind me.

"Well, if it isn't the pervert again."

I stood and turned. Tony was swaying more than he had been earlier. Clearly he'd made full use of the hospitality tent. "Haven't you said enough, Tony?"

"Not yet. "People began to turn. "I thought I'd tell you the truth about your sainted brother. He was certainly no saint. Did you know he ran a protection racket at school? He used to take money off the smaller kids."

I glanced around. "This isn't the place, Tony."

"Of course, it's the place. People should know the truth. He told me, you know. He told me the farm was failing and how he intended to kill himself for the insurance money. He couldn't face losing everything. He was a useless farmer."

I gritted my teeth and stared at him, chin up. I wasn't going to let him intimidate me. "And you're a liar. You've always been a liar. I've often wondered what happened on that awful day myself and, hearing those words from you, convinces me even more that it was an accident."

Jed appeared at my side and touched my arm. "You were always a bully, Tony. And bullies are cowards."

Tony swayed. "Oh look. Another pervert. You wouldn't dare lay a hand on me. I remember flushing your head down the loo. You cried like a baby."

Jed moved towards him.

"Don't," I warned. "He's not worth it."

"Beth," I turned to see Chrissy with Rob and Ingrid.

"And oh wow, here's the girlfriend."

Chrissy stood next to me. "What's his problem?"

"I'll tell you what his problem is," Jed said. "His wife and family buggered off to New Zealand because they couldn't stand him anymore, and Janice has a new girlfriend. He's also about to lose his business and he owes thousands."

Tony moved closer, arms flailing. "I'll shut you up, you queer bastard." He stumbled. By now quite a crowd had gathered. In the distance, I saw stewards heading our way. I didn't notice Chrissy moving to stand in front of me.

"I think you need to go," she said.

"Who the fuck are you to tell me what to do—some interloper from the south?"

Chrissy stood her ground as he moved closer. "Don't make me do this," she said.

"Chrissy, leave it. He's a big bloke and he's drunk."

Without warning, Tony moved forward and raised his hands. Things happened so quickly, but somehow Tony ended up on his back on the ground shouting. I stared. Chrissy had thrown him over her shoulder as if he weighed nothing and now stood above him brushing her hands together.

"Not lost it then, sis," Rob said.

I glanced over at him.

"We did judo as kids," he explained. "Our dad runs a club. We're both black belts. Chrissy could have fought for England in the Commonwealth Games. It's all about balance taking on someone his size."

Jed spoke to the stewards while I hugged Chrissy. "You didn't tell me you were a martial arts expert."

"It's not something I think about now, but I suppose you don't forget. He seems like a nasty piece of work with a large chip on his shoulder."

"He is." The stewards led Tony away and gradually people lost interest. "You'd better get back in there," I said to Jed.

Rob took out two collapsing stools from his bag and they sat with Chrissy and me. "Are you all right?" he asked. "We couldn't help hearing what he said."

Chrissy put her arm around my waist. I loved the feel of her touch. "He was my brother's friend and brought out the worst in him. I'd like to claim Neil was easily led, but there was a streak of something in him too. I loved him but he could be arrogant. I knew the farm was failing, and I've always wondered about the accident, but I know Tony would only say those words to hurt me. Neil loved the farm. I've never doubted that, and above all else he loved the animals. He and Tony fell out over something just before he died, which is why I know he didn't talk to him. Tony kicked out at Jake, Neil's dog. Hurting animals was something Neil wouldn't countenance. The last time I saw him we talked. He apologised for a lot of what he'd done. I told him I'd help with the finances."

Chrissy handed me a tissue.

"And now the results of the mother and baby section for Highland cattle."

We all turned at the voice from the loud-speaker. The judge presented the third and second places.

"And finally, the winner is Nethering Farm with Bonnie and Belle, presented by Jed Atherton."

We clapped and cheered—our first win of the show. I waved at Jed. The prize money would come in handy.

"Mum, are you okay?" Amy and Ralph appeared out of nowhere. "Someone said Chrissy put some drunk on the floor after an incident."

I stood and hugged her. "Don't worry. It's all over now. I'll tell you later. We're going to have lunch then watch you and Ralph perform before I have to do my stint on the ice cream van. We've already won a prize, so now it's your turn."

Lunch was savoury pancakes from a stall, then we made our

way to the agility course. Amy had been practising for months on the obstacles she'd created in one of our fields. Ralph was a natural and he loved a challenge. We watched the first ten contenders, then it was Amy and Ralph. They made no mistakes and whizzed around. Ralph moved like liquid between the poles smiling throughout. Now it was a matter of waiting. Each of the other contestants, as far as my timings showed, didn't beat their time. At the end of the contest, we waited. When Amy's name was announced as the winner things had definitely taken a turn for the better. Amy brought her prize to show us, and Ralph got cuddles from everyone.

By ten that night, I was yawning, and we still had another two days. I lay in bed with Chrissy.

"I'm sorry I can't come again," Chrissy said. "Though hopefully, your days will be less eventful. Claire and I have appointments. One woman is coming from North Wales."

"You must be pleased," I said. "It's been a success—the shop, I mean."

"So far. The income is steady. I can pay my landlady, and my rent."

"About that," I said. "I wondered, if when your contract is up, you'd consider moving in with me. You spend so much time here anyway. What do you think?"

Chrissy rolled over on top of me and kissed me hard. I wrapped my arms around her. When we pulled apart, she was grinning from ear to ear. "I take it that's a yes," I said, returning the smile.

"Of course it's a yes. I love you, and I can't think of anything better than going to sleep with you every night and waking up with you every morning."

"Even if the alarm goes off at five-thirty every morning, and during lambing season when no one gets any sleep?"

Chrissy snuggled beside me. "Even then. I can't wait to see all the lambs born." She closed her eyes while I stared at the ceiling.

It had been a wonderful day.

# Epilogue - Chrissy

## SIX MONTHS LATER – NEW YEAR'S EVE

I couldn't believe I was reading in bed on New Year's Eve, but here I was waiting for Beth to return from lambing. They lambed indoors to make sure of a constant supply of milk for processing. It meant, since before Christmas, they'd been busy. The opening and closing of the front door and footsteps on the stairs told me Beth had returned. I lifted my head then sniffed the air.

"Yes, I know, I stink. One of the sheep with triplets went into labour. All safely delivered but we had to try to get another sheep to take the spare. Birth is a messy business. Thank goodness for wellies and waterproof trousers."

"Did the lamb take?" I'd become quite knowledgeable about farming practices and knew sheep had two teats, unlike cows. A few ewes had triplets, so they always attempted to get a sheep with one lamb to take the other on. It was a complicated process but saved a lot of hand- rearing.

"It did, thankfully. We got the first feed from the mother, so everything went well. We still have a few ewes carrying three." I knew each sheep was scanned and labelled. Preparation for lambing was meticulous, from judging feed for each ewe to shaving their bottoms before the process started. Here they got the ewes indoors and kept the lambs with their mothers for up to sixty days. I had to remind myself occasionally that farming is a business.

"I'm heading for the shower. Care to join me?"

I wasn't going to turn down such an offer. Beth stripped the rest of her clothes and threw them into the basket. I hurried to follow her into the spacious cubicle.

"Let me wash you," I said, squeezing gel on a sponge. The shower had a fold-down seat left over from when Beth's parents used it. I did Beth's shoulders then sat down, did her back, then her front. The seat left my face level with her breasts. I may have spent more than a little time making sure they were clean. Beth smiled at me. I loved the way they moved and how I could squeeze then together. Her nipples were a dusky pink. I licked my lips then moved one hand to wash between her legs.

"You're being thorough."

"I like to do a good job. After all, we can't have you smelling of sheep at the wedding tomorrow."

"No. All I need is a good night's sleep."

I placed the sponge to one side. "Perhaps I can help." I stared into her blue eyes then slipped my hand between her thighs and found her clit. I leaned forward and took a nipple between my lips. We stared at each other as I pressed with my fingers. I was rewarded with a groan from Beth. I sucked harder brushing my teeth over the nub.

"Shit, you're good. Mmm, feels wonderful." She tensed. "Not going to take long." She rested her arms on my shoulders for balance and moved her feet apart. Her head went back, sending her hair tumbling across her shoulders.

"Oh yes, a little to the left. Oh yeah—there. So close. Don't stop." Moisture flooded my hand. I kept going until she grabbed my shoulders much harder, then pulled away and sponged my hand.

"Sit," I said. We swapped positions. She looked tired.

"Let's go to bed," I said. "You dry yourself off and I'll make us a hot chocolate. So bloody rock and roll for a New Year's Eve."

"I'll try not to fall asleep while I wait."

I returned to find Beth sat up staring at her laptop. "Just checking the lambing rota," she said. "Ned is in charge tomorrow as Jed is at the wedding with us. I'll wash my hair tomorrow. You all right?"

I placed the mugs at the side of the bed and slipped under the duvet. I knew what she meant. "I'm fine," I said, sipping the sweet chocolate. I glanced at the clock. "We've missed the New Year." I leaned over and kissed her. "Happy New Year."

"So much has changed," Beth said.

"For the better?" I asked.

Beth laughed. I loved the sound. "Stop fishing for compliments. You know it's for the better. The farm is doing well. The ice cream is selling better than we could have hoped for. So far, we've only lost one lamb, and we've a wedding to go to tomorrow —such a nice way to start the year."

We sipped our drinks and enjoyed the London fireworks online. Ralph snuck in through the door and jumped onto the bottom of the bed. He stared at us plaintively.

"Just this once," Beth said for the umpteenth time. He

missed Amy now she was away at university. It didn't take long for any of us to fall asleep.

I woke at six-thirty to find the space next to me was already empty. It was still pitch-black outside. I frowned. Beth supposedly had the day off, but I knew she'd help if necessary. Most ewes managed without help, but another multiple birth could have happened. I switched on the light and got ready for the day, leaving my outfit hanging over the door for now. I found Beth in the kitchen clutching a large mug of tea and staring at a huge spreadsheet on her laptop.

"Sorry," she said. "Body clock doesn't switch off, so I thought I'd update the records. It's been a good year so far."

I switched on the kettle and put bread in the toaster. "Have you heard from Amy?"

"Yes. She texted she would be here by ten. Tash is driving them over. Ralph will be happy to see her." Currently, the border collie was asleep in his basket next to the Aga. .

"And your mum?" I was terrified of meeting the formidable Sarah Nethering.

"Her flight arrived on time last night. She stayed at a hotel at the airport. Pierre is driving them this morning. She's keen to meet you. She says she might need a wedding dress herself."

I raised my eyebrows. "Really? Well, I'm sure I could find something for her." I made the tea and buttered the toast then sat at the table. "The ceremony is at midday. I'll be going after I've eaten to help the bride and bridesmaids get ready. If I say so myself, the dress is stunning."

"At least they have a venue, and they found a celebrant ready to work on New Year's Day. I did wonder about having weddings here once, but we'd need to build a space and there are several other venues locally. I didn't want to step on anyone's toes. I might pop over to the barn to check on overnight after I've collected the eggs and fed the chickens. Apparently, it's going to be bright but cold today. It might be icy underfoot."

"I left the car close by, but I'll be wearing my boots until I'm indoors. I'm not taking any chances." I wiped the toast crumbs from my face and finished my drink. "Right. I'd better get my suit and get going." I stood, kissed the top of Beth's head, and scooted upstairs. Outside, a hint of colour on the horizon indicated the sun was on the rise. I double-checked I had everything. By the time I returned downstairs the kitchen was empty. I grabbed my make-up case and carefully made my way to my car. Ice covered the windscreen, and it took a while to defrost. Beth appeared with Ralph at her side, carrying the egg basket. I wound the window down.

"I'll see you in a few hours," I said.

"Take care on the bends. It could be slippery and there won't have been much traffic to warm up the roads. Hopefully, the gritters were out."

"I'll text you to say I'm there.

The journey didn't take long, and I drove carefully. I turned into the car park at the back of Nethering Inn to see Jan standing at the back door. He hurried towards me.

"I'm on duty," he said. "I've salted everywhere, but the last thing we need is someone having a fall today."

I handed him my case then gathered everything else. "How is she?" I asked.

"Nervous, but a Buck's Fizz or two will help. Mum is running around checking everything, and Dad is cooking up a storm in the kitchen bossing the caterers and wishing his own staff were there. It's going to be a long day."

Once inside, I made my way upstairs to the private quarters. I knocked on the door. "It's me."

"Come in."

I opened the door to find Claire and her friend Tess sipping drinks out of champagne flutes. I laughed. "Dutch courage?" I asked.

Claire smiled. She was radiant—everything a bride should be on her wedding day. "Would you like some?" she asked.

"Maybe later. I need a steady hand, or you'll end up looking like a panda. We've two hours to get you ready."

By eleven-thirty, we were all dressed. "Beautiful," I said to Claire when she stood ready to go. She'd chosen a simple white dress with a corseted bodice and wide satin skirt. A faux fur trim covered the neckline and over the top of the sleeves, leaving her shoulders bare. Her veil was held on with a fur headband. Tess wore an ice-blue dress that seemed to shimmer when she moved. I wore a suit—three piece with a blouse and low heels in dark purple. Finally, we were ready. Karen had been in and out a few times.

She appeared with fifteen minutes to go. "Oh, my darling," she said, taking Claire's hands. "I'm so proud of you and all you've achieved this year. Everyone is here and waiting."

"Are you decent?"

"Yes," we chorused.

George stepped into the room, having swapped his cooking gear for a dapper morning suit in grey. Tears welled in his eyes.

"I think we should leave them to it," I said, remembering my own wedding day. Once downstairs, we took our seats , leaving Tess to wait at the door for the bride.

"That outfit suits you, even though it's not midnight blue," I said to Beth. Today she wore a lavender dress. On her other side sat Sarah and her handsome beau, Pierre. We nodded to each other. My stomach swirled at the thought of talking to my girlfriend's mother. After all, I was the woman who had changed the way she thought of herself.

The room was full. Matt and his best man stood at the front dressed in their morning suits. Every so often Matt glanced backwards. I assumed it was his family on the front row of the other side of the aisle. Organising the wedding hadn't been a logistical nightmare as the bride lived in a wedding venue, but the fact Matt had proposed, and Claire had decided she wanted to start the new year as a wife had given them less than a month to organise everything. Karen and George had called in favours all over the place. It also helped Claire had many dresses to choose from.

The music began dead on midday. Doors at the back opened and Tess stepped through, followed by Claire and her father. We listened to the celebrant saying her piece then the vows. Beth took my hand in hers. In front of us, Karen dabbed her eyes every so often. Soon it was over, and the happy couple walked down the aisle. Everyone headed to the lounge bar while staff bustled away, changing the room from a wedding venue to a wedding breakfast venue. Later everything would be moved again to create a dancefloor. They were well-rehearsed.

For a couple of hours, we ate and drank then listened to the speeches. During the meal, Sarah interrogated me about my family, where I was from, my divorce, and my intentions.

I swallowed more wine.

Beth leaned over the table. "For goodness' sake, Mum. I'm surprised you're not shining a light on Chrissy."

"I'm thinking of you, darling. After all, Chrissy here has always been a lesbian, but you're new at it."

Beth's face turned a deeper shade of red than I thought possible.

"She's getting in a fair bit of practice though," Jed whispered none-too-quietly to Lars.

"And I believe you're also stepping out with a girlfriend, Amy. You'd better treat me right, Pierre, or I might have to find out what's so exciting to my daughter and granddaughter both —mind you, there was a time in school once—"

"Mum? Really?"

"Oh, darling. The girls at my boarding school were at it all the time. Your generation didn't invent sex you know."

Next to me, Jed burst out laughing. He held his glass aloft. "To the gays," he said. Everyone took hold of their glasses and joined in.

By mid-afternoon, everyone was ready to move though we were all stuffed with gorgeous food, and many had already had their fair share of wine. One by one, until only the top table was left, everything was cleared, leaving a space in the centre of the room. The DJ had already set up his equipment.

"And now could everyone welcome Claire and Matt to the floor for their first dance as a married couple. The opening chords of *All of Me* sounded from the speakers on either side of the room. Matt took Claire in his arms, and they danced. Soon others joined them, and the dance floor filled.

"Care to join everyone?" I asked Beth.

"I'd love to."

We joined the throng, and no one bat an eyelid as we danced together alongside Jed and Lars.

The dancing, and drinking continued for hours. Outside it was dark again. All of the glamping pods had been booked by wedding guests and Beth had given out the keys earlier. I suspected the local taxi driver would be doing a roaring trade charging double time to take people to where they were staying for the night.

Claire sat next to me and Beth. "Have you had a good time?" she asked grinning. "I'm having a lush day. Matt uses lush all the time. It's such a lush word." She glanced over to where Matt stood talking with his family. "I'm so lucky. He's everything I've ever wanted—so kind and thoughtful." She leaned closer. "And he's great in bed." She giggled.

"Sorry. I've had a few. I mean it's not like I've got to go far tonight—just up the stairs then tomorrow we're off to New Zealand. I can't wait to see where they filmed *Lord of the Rings*. Matt loves it too and he has family there. I wish we had longer than two weeks. I'm sorry to leave you in the lurch."

"That's all right," I said, patting her arm.

She stared at me then at Beth. "You two could get married, you know. Both of you being divorced doesn't mean anything."

"Maybe," I said glancing at Beth. "Would you like to?"

"Are you asking? Being a farmer's wife will mean lots of early mornings and working with sheep, lambs, cattle, chickens, Jed, and living with the smell of manure. It's not a glamorous life.

*Am I?* "Yes, I think I am asking."

Beth placed a hand either side of my face and kissed me. "Then I'd love to. And I know the exact dress I would choose to wear, in the exact shade of midnight blue."

I grinned. "I love you," I said, wanting to pinch myself. This time last year seemed so long ago, and so much had changed. People close enough to hear the conversation cheered.

"And I," said Beth. "I love you too.

231

# Author's Note

This story is my first full length f/f romance. I wanted to write a story about a larger woman. I wanted to write about someone who faces challenges and takes on what life throws at her. Beth is that character. She is strong and resourceful, but also ready to take risks. Chrissy too, has taken a chance and left her previous life behind.

Various people have helped along the way and given me ideas. As always, Cath has listened to me talk about the characters as if they are real people. The editing was done by the wonderful Sue Laybourn, who gave me good advice, and the cover by the talented Garrett Leigh of Black Jazz Design.

Lastly, thank you for reading this. If you enjoyed the story, I'd be grateful for a review it as I'm a new voice in sapphic fiction, and it's often difficult to be seen when you take a risk and enter a new world.

# About Alexa Milne

Originally from South Wales, Alexa has lived in the Northwest of England for over forty years. Now retired, after a long career in teaching, she devotes her time to her obsessions.

Alexa began writing when her favourite character was killed in her favourite show. After producing a lot of fanfiction, she ventured into original writing.

She is currently owned by a mad cat and spends her time writing about the men and women in her head, watching her favourite television programmes, and usually crying over her favourite football teams.

# Also by Alexa Milne

## Novels

Sporting Chance

Comfort Zone

My Highland Cowboy

Two for the Road

His Perfect Companion

Of Dungarees, Wellies, and Wedding Dresses

## The Call of Home Series

Choosing Home

Returning Home

Staying Home

## Finding Family Series

Half Empty

Half Full

Brimming Over

## The Wanderlings Series

The Cat Who Came in From the Cold

The Cat Who Went into the Woods

The Cat Who Learned How to Fly (coming next year)

## Novellas

More Than This

A String of Lights

## Short Stories

Stay

Not Every Time

A Bell Rings

The Matchmaker